2012

D0404604

Ryder scoo
racing back a
another explosion rocked the house.

It threw him to his knees, but he kept his arms tight around Shelby's soft, limp body.

"What happened?" she gasped, coughing on the acrid fumes.

"Explosion."

"Maureen's in there!" She shoved away, jumped to her feet and ran straight back toward the inferno.

He followed, heat searing his cheeks. "There's nothing we can do to help her."

She turned, tears trekking down her cheeks. Near her temple was a deep cut that oozed blood. She didn't seem to feel the pain of it. Didn't seem to know she was hurt.

Memories threatened to overtake Ryder. He shoved the images down deep as fire continued to lick along the facade of the house.

Shelby stopped in her tracks, her face lit by flames and stained with soot.

Ryder took her arm and urged her to the front yard. There might be another explosion, and he didn't want Shelby anywhere near the building if there was.

Books by Shirlee McCoy

Love Inspired Suspense

Die Before Nightfall
Even in the Darkness
When Silence Falls
Little Girl Lost
Valley of Shadows
Stranger in the Shadows
Missing Persons
Lakeview Protector
*The Guardian's Mission
*The Protector's Promise
Cold Case Murder
*The Defender's Duty
†Running for Cover
Deadly Vows
†Running Scared

†Running Blind
Out of Time
†Lone Defender
†Private Eye Protector
The Lawman's Legacy
†Undercover Bodyguard

Love Inspired Single Title

Still Waters

*The Sinclair Brothers
†Heroes for Hire

SHIRLEE McCOY

has always loved making up stories. As a child, she daydreamed elaborate tales in which she was the heroine—gutsy, strong and invincible. Though she soon grew out of her superhero fantasies, her love for storytelling never diminished. She knew early that she wanted to write inspirational fiction, and she began writing her first novel when she was a teenager. Still, it wasn't until her third son was born that she truly began pursuing her dream of being published. Three years later, she sold her first book. Now a busy mother of five, Shirlee is a homeschool mom by day and an inspirational author by night. She and her husband and children live in the Pacific Northwest and share their house with a dog, two cats and a bird. You can visit her website, www.shirleemccoy.com, or email her at shirlee@shirleemccoy.com.

Shirlee McCoy

UNDERCOVER BODYGUARD

Love Inspired

If you purchased this book without a cover you should be aware
that this book is stolen property. It was reported as "unsold and
destroyed" to the publisher, and neither the author nor the
publisher has received any payment for this "stripped book."

Recycling programs
for this product may
not exist in your area.

LOVE INSPIRED BOOKS

ISBN-13: 978-0-373-67505-0

UNDERCOVER BODYGUARD

Copyright © 2012 by Shirlee McCoy

All rights reserved. Except for use in any review, the reproduction
or utilization of this work in whole or in part in any form by any
electronic, mechanical or other means, now known or hereafter
invented, including xerography, photocopying and recording, or in
any information storage or retrieval system, is forbidden without
the written permission of the editorial office, Love Inspired Books,
233 Broadway, New York, NY 10279 U.S.A.

This is a work of fiction. Names, characters, places and incidents are
either the product of the author's imagination or are used fictitiously, and
any resemblance to actual persons, living or dead, business establishments,
events or locales is entirely coincidental.

This edition published by arrangement with Love Inspired Books.

® and TM are trademarks of Love Inspired Books, used under license.
Trademarks indicated with ® are registered in the United States Patent
and Trademark Office, the Canadian Trade Marks Office and in other
countries.

www.LoveInspiredBooks.com

Printed in U.S.A.

Because you are my help,
I sing in the shadow of your wings.
My soul clings to you; your right hand upholds me.
—*Psalms* 63:7–8

To my friends at An Orphan's Wish who work tirelessly to shower His love on China's orphaned children. May God continue to bless your efforts.

ONE

"Come on, Old Blue, don't fail me now!" Shelby Simons turned the key in the ignition of her 1958 Cadillac and prayed that *this* time, the engine would turn over.

It didn't, of course.

That would have made her morning just a little too easy.

"Fine. Stay here. I can walk the four blocks to Maureen Lewis's place," she grumbled.

She grabbed two large bakery boxes from the backseat and closed Old Blue's door with a little too much force. She loved the car, but it was as fickle as its original owner, Grandma Beulah, had been.

The scent of chocolate wafted from the boxes as Shelby picked her way across the bakery's empty parking lot, and her stomach growled. Stupid diet. Eight days of starving herself, and she still could barely fit into the little black dress her sister had sent from Paris.

But Shelby *would* fit into it before the Spokane

Business Association's black-tie dinner that she'd planned to attend with Andrew Willis.

Andrew, her ex-fiancé, who'd promised her a million dreams and given her nothing but lies.

Now, he'd be attending the function with Stephanie Parsons, and Shelby would be going alone, because there was no way she was going to stay home moping about her newly single status. Sure, she'd been planning a wedding two short months ago, but God had had other plans, and Shelby had to believe they were better than the ones she'd made for herself.

Marriage.

Family.

Forever with someone who loved her.

She sighed, hefting the bakery boxes a little higher and doing her best to ignore the fragrant aroma that drifted from them. Maureen would be pleased with the assortment of pastries Shelby was providing for the early-morning kickoff to Maureen's birthday bash. She'd invited Shelby to attend the breakfast *and* the New York shopping spree she and her closest friends were going on afterward, but unlike Maureen, Shelby wasn't a bestselling true-crime writer with plenty of money to throw around. She had bills to pay and a business to run. Being at the bakery she'd opened five years ago was the only way to do it. Though, she had to admit, flying to New York to shop sounded like a lot more fun.

She walked up South Hill, heading toward 21st Street, the quiet morning making her feel more lonely than usual. Two months, and she was over Andrew. If she were honest, she'd admit that she'd been over him two *minutes* after she'd caught him kissing Stephanie and broken their engagement. But she still craved the connection she'd had with him, still missed having someone she could call when she was walking up a dark street by herself and felt vulnerable and alone. Not that Andrew would have appreciated an early-morning call, but she'd always thought that once they were married…

She cut the thought off before it could form.

She hadn't agreed to marry him because she'd thought she could change him. She'd agreed because she'd thought she'd loved him. More importantly, she'd thought he had loved her.

Obviously, she'd been wrong on both counts.

If she'd loved him, her heart would still be broken.

If he'd loved her, he wouldn't have fallen for Stephanie while he was engaged to Shelby.

Shelby frowned, not sure why she was thinking about Andrew. She had plenty on her plate without worrying about the past. She had three deliveries to make and a car that wouldn't start. Maybe Maureen would lend her one of the three cars she owned. *If* Shelby arrived on time. Maureen was a stickler for punctuality, and if Shelby was even a minute late making the 5:20 delivery, Maureen would not be happy.

She picked up her pace. One more block. She could do that in three minutes. Which was exactly how much time she had left. Up ahead, a dark figure bounded around the corner of Maureen's street, jogging toward Shelby with a swift pace that bordered on a run.

She stepped off the sidewalk as he neared, her heart doing a funny little dance. Dark sunglasses on a nondescript face, a jacket zipped up to his neck, a hood pulled over his hair—he looked like trouble.

Why else would he be wearing sunglasses before dawn?

Why else would he have black leather gloves on his hands?

She fished her cell phone from her apron pocket, knowing the battery was dead and wishing she'd remembered to charge it *before* a guy who looked like a serial killer jogged by. She pressed the phone to her ear anyway, holding an imaginary conversation and praying he would just keep going.

He did, but she couldn't shake the fear that shivered along her spine as he turned his head, seemed to look right at her.

Shelby clutched the boxes a little closer, watching his progress as he approached 20th Street.

Should she knock on someone's door and ask to use a phone?

What would she say if she did?

There's a guy jogging down South Hill wear-

ing gloves and sunglasses and looking scary didn't
seem all that compelling.

He stopped abruptly, stood in the shadows of the
old manor house that some development company
was restoring. Turned to face her. He was a block
away, but she could feel his eyes behind those dark
glasses, feel them staring straight into hers. Her
heart thrummed painfully as he took a step toward
her.

One step, but she had a feeling he planned to take
more.

Terror froze her in place, every nightmare she'd
ever had coming true as he took another step.

A car passed, its lights splashing over Shelby,
drawing her attention away from the approaching
threat for a split second. When she looked back, the
man had disappeared.

She wanted to believe he'd turned down
20th Street and gone on his way, but she could
still feel his gaze, hot and ugly and terrifying. She
stepped back, afraid to turn her back to the unseen
threat, worried that he'd be on her before she even
knew he was coming.

Never turn your back on a predator.

That's what Grandma Beulah had always said,
but then, Beulah had been a B movie actress and
had spent more time in Beverly Hills than the great
outdoors. Shelby couldn't claim to know much more
than Beulah had about predators, but she knew that

standing around waiting for a creepy jogger to lunge from the shadows wasn't going to do her any good.

She pivoted and took off, glancing back and seeing nothing. She was still terrified, still sure she could feel him breathing down her neck, and she half expected to be tackled from behind at any second.

She turned down Maureen's street. Five houses to go, and she could ring Maureen's doorbell, see her friend's cheerful smile. Maybe then she'd be able to convince herself that Sunglasses Guy was nothing more than an early-morning jogger.

An engine revved and headlights splashed across the cracked sidewalk, spilling onto lush yards filled with blooming daffodils and flowering shrubs. Shelby glanced over her shoulder, spotted a black Hummer rolling along the street. There was no one on the sidewalk. No hint that she'd been chased or that her fear was well-founded. She slowed to a walk, lungs burning, heart thundering as she waited for the Hummer to pass.

It pulled up beside her, going so slowly she could easily have outrun it. Big and black with tinted windows, it had plenty of room in the back to stuff a woman.

Had Sunglasses Guy come after her?

Her pulse jumped at the thought. She couldn't see through the tinted glass, but she was sure she felt his dark gaze. She ran the last few steps to Maureen's driveway, her hair standing on end when the

Hummer pulled in behind her. The driver's door opened, and Shelby didn't wait to see if Sunglasses Guy would get out. She dropped the pastries and ran for Maureen's door, her pulse jumping as someone snagged the back of her apron and pulled her to a stop.

She screamed, fists swinging, lungs filling for another scream.

"Cool it, Shelby Ann. I'm not in the mood to have my nose broken." The voice was familiar, but she swung again anyway, her knuckles brushing a firm jaw.

"I said, cool it." He grabbed her hand, held it in a grip that she couldn't loosen no matter how desperately she tried.

"Let me go!" she yelled, looking up, up and *up* into the face of her attacker.

The *familiar* face of her attacker.

She knew him!

Not Sunglasses Guy.

Hercules. The muscular, too-good-looking-to-be-for-real guy who'd been coming into Just Desserts at the crack of dawn every morning for the past four months, watching her intently as she filled his order. Two doughnuts and a large coffee. Black. To go. She'd noticed him the first day he'd walked into the bakery, and she'd been noticing him ever since. What woman wouldn't? The guy should be on the front cover of a bodybuilder magazine.

"What are *you* doing here?" She managed to sputter, and he raised an eyebrow.

"Looking for you."

"Well, you found me *and* scared me, and now I've ruined three dozen pastries." Her voice shook as she tugged away. "Maureen is *not* going to be happy."

"I'm sure they're salvageable." He lifted the boxes, opened the one on the top and frowned. "Some of them."

"*None* of them. I'm going to have to go back for more." She huffed, eyeing the smashed tops of several muffins, her pulse racing for a reason that had nothing to do with fear and everything to do with the man standing beside her. There was just something about his dark, knowing gaze that unbalanced her, and having him there, talking to her, looking straight into her eyes, studying her face...

Unbalanced was exactly how she felt.

She frowned, pulling the boxes from his hands. "You said you were looking for me. Did Dottie send you?" Dottie had been part of Shelby's life for as long as she could remember. A good friend of Beulah's, she'd shown up at the bakery a week after Beulah's funeral, and she'd been hanging around ever since.

"She said you didn't take your car out for the delivery, and she was worried about you walking here alone."

"My car wouldn't start, so I didn't have much of a choice."

"Next time, call someone to give you a ride."

"Before dawn? Who would I call?" she asked, and he shrugged.

"A friend. Family. Someone who can make sure you get where you're going and back safely."

"I've been getting where I'm going and back safely for years, Herc—" She stopped short of calling him what she'd been calling him in her head since the first day she'd seen him. "I guess you have me at a disadvantage. You know my name, but I don't know yours."

"Ryder Malone."

"Well, like I said, Ryder, I've been running my own business and getting by just fine for five years. I'm not sure what possessed Dottie to worry now, but you can go back to what you were doing before she sent you out looking for me." She took a step toward Maureen's door, but Ryder pulled her up short.

"What I was doing was waiting for my doughnuts and coffee. Dottie won't sell them to me until I get you back to the bakery in one piece, so going back to what I was doing isn't going to accomplish anything."

"Oh, for goodness' sake! What is that woman up to now?" she muttered, shoving the boxes toward him. "Here. Hold these. I'll tell Maureen that I need to run back to the bakery. If you don't mind giving me a ride, we should be able to get things cleared up pretty quickly and get you on your way."

"No problem." He took a ruined muffin from the top box and bit into it. "Still tastes great. Are you sure your customer won't—"

"I'm sure." She cut him off, anxious to give Maureen the bad news and get back to the bakery. She had too much to do to waste time, and she planned to tell Dottie that. Of all the things the woman had done in the four years she'd been working at the bakery, sending Ryder Malone out searching for Shelby took the cake.

A sad attempt at matchmaking. That's what it was, and Shelby did *not* have the patience for it.

She marched to Maureen's front door, bracing herself for the tantrum she knew was coming. As much as she liked the vivacious, spontaneous fifty-year-old, Shelby thought Maureen was a little too much like her mother and sister. Sweet but spoiled. Kind, as long as things were going her way.

Right now, things were not going Maureen's way, and Shelby expected to hear about it.

She rang the doorbell of the beautiful Victorian, glancing at her watch as she did so. Already five minutes late, and she still had to return to the bakery to get new product. Maureen was *not* going to be happy.

As a matter of fact, Shelby was surprised she hadn't already opened the door and demanded an explanation. Now that she thought about it, Shelby was surprised there were no lights on, no sign that Maureen was getting ready for her fiftieth birthday celebration. An early breakfast, a limo ride to the airport and an early flight out to New York City.

Be there by 5:20 a.m., Shelby. Not a minute later. Our flight leaves at 8:30, and the girls will be showing up on my doorstep at 6:00 expecting a birthday breakfast to die for.

Maureen's words rang in Shelby's ears, anxiety simmering in her stomach as she peered into the narrow window beside the door. Nothing. Not even a hint of movement.

Concerned, she rang the doorbell again and heard something. A muffled sound that came from deep within the house.

And then the world exploded.

Glass sprayed from the windows to either side of the door. Heat blazed from flames that shot from somewhere.

Everywhere.

Another explosion, and she was flying, spinning, hurtling through space. Away from the burning door. Away from the shattered glass. Away from the lightening morning and deep blue sky. Flying and whirling into darkness so black and deep she knew she'd never escape it.

TWO

The force of the explosion knocked Ryder Malone from his feet. He went down hard, his thigh cramping, his pulse racing, a thousand memories trying to drag him into the past. He ignored them, jumping to his feet and running across the grass that separated him from Shelby Simons. Pretty, amusing, uncomplicated Shelby Simons. Owner of the only bakery in town that knew how to make a doughnut right.

Owner of the sweetest smile he'd seen in years.

She intrigued him. Her quiet joy, her easy humor, the comfortable way she interacted with the people who entered her bakery, all those qualities set to a backdrop of quiet beauty and stunning blue eyes.

Now, she lay facedown on the ground, bits of shingle and wood falling around her like glowing confetti. They coated her back and her thick dark hair, covered the ground around her prone figure. Flames shot from broken windows on either side of the thick wood door she'd been standing in front of. A few inches to the left or right, and she'd have been sliced to bits.

He brushed an ember from silky curls, felt the pulse point in her neck. It beat slow and steady.

Alive.

No time to check for injuries. Not with the fire raging out of control and the house groaning beneath the onslaught of flames.

He scooped her up, racing back across the yard as another explosion rocked the house. It threw him to his knees, but he kept his arms tight around Shelby's soft, limp body.

Neighbors spilled from their homes, frantic cries mixing with the roar of the blaze that consumed the beautiful Victorian, the sounds background noise to Ryder's racing thoughts. He'd seen explosions, felt them, lived through them. He hadn't expected one in Spokane. Not on a sleepy spring morning.

"Shelby?" He brushed thick hair from her cheek, and she shifted, her eyes slowly opening.

"What happened?" She gasped, coughing on the acrid fumes that poured from the burning shell of the old house.

"Some kind of explosion."

"Explosion? Maureen!" She shoved away, jumped to her feet and ran straight back toward the inferno.

He snagged the bow of her apron, pulling her to a stop, and she swung around, her eyes wide with horror. "Maureen is in there."

"There's nothing we can do for her now," he said truthfully, and she yanked from his hold, spun away, running toward the house again.

He followed, heat searing his cheeks as flames whooshed through the roof and windows, consuming wood and melting wiring, the scent suffocating.

"Shelby! She's dead. There's nothing we can do to help her," he shouted, grabbing her apron again.

"She's my friend. I have to try."

"And kill yourself in the process? I can't let you do that." He wouldn't let her do that, but she turned, tears trekking down her cheeks, leaving white trails in her soot-stained face. A large knot peeked out from beneath silky curls near her temple, the swollen flesh surrounding a deep cut that oozed blood. She didn't seem to feel the pain of it. Didn't seem to know she was hurt.

"It's her birthday, Ryder. Her fiftieth. She can't be dead."

He touched her cheek, tried to make her see the futility of the situation. "People die on their birthdays all the time."

"I know, but that doesn't mean Maureen is dead. Maybe she survived the explosion. Maybe she's upstairs, trying to find a way through the smoke and flames. I can't just stand here and watch her house burn around her."

"Shelby—"

She'd turned away again, racing around to the back of the house, dark hair glowing gold in the firelight.

He followed, his thigh aching, the memories threatening to overtake him.

Smoke.

Flames.

His comrades consumed by it.

Ryder consumed.

He shoved the images down deep, refusing them the way he had so many times in the six years since an explosive device had taken the lives of four of the ten navy SEALs who'd been sent to hunt a high-level terrorist in Afghanistan.

Fire licked along the facade of the house, blazing across the back-porch roof, snapping and crackling as it ate its way up wood posts. Engulfed, the back door offered no hope of entry, the shattered windows only serving as a conduit for black smoke and red-gold flames to pour out.

Death had come calling, and it had taken every living thing in its path.

Shelby stopped in her tracks, her face lit by flames.

"She really is dead, isn't she?" she asked quietly, the words barely carrying over the fire's crackling hiss. Tears streamed down her cheeks, mixing with blood and soot, but her voice was steady, her gaze direct.

"Yes."

"It's her birthday." She repeated the information as if doing so would somehow change what had happened to her friend.

"I know. Come on." He took her arm, urging her to the front yard. Two explosions had already rocked the house. There might be another, and he didn't want Shelby anywhere near the building if there was.

Three fire trucks were parked at the curb, firefighters hooking a hose to the hydrant across the street. The ordered chaos of the scene strummed along Ryder's nerves, making him anxious and antsy. He'd wanted a couple of doughnuts and some coffee, and he'd gotten trouble instead. Not a good morning. That was for sure.

He hurried Shelby across the street, and a tall, thin firefighter stopped them there, his gaze jumping from Ryder to Shelby.

"You okay, folks?" he asked.

"We're fine, but my friend Maureen..." Shelby didn't finish.

"Is she inside?"

"Yes."

"Anyone else in there that you know of?"

"No. She lived alone."

"Okay. We'll do what we can to find her, but it doesn't look good."

"I know." Shelby offered a watery smile, and Ryder's heart constricted, the feeling both surprising and uncomfortable. He'd noticed Shelby and her sweet smile every time he'd gone into her bakery, but noticing wasn't the same as feeling something for her.

And he *was* feeling.

Sympathy, concern, curiosity about the woman who seemed both strong and vulnerable.

"I'm going to send an EMT over. You need to get the cut on your head looked at." The firefighter hurried away, and Shelby put a hand to her temple, fingering the lump that still oozed blood.

"It doesn't even hurt," she said, shivering as she looked at her bloodied fingers.

"Shock will do that to you. Here." Ryder shrugged out of his jacket and draped it around her shoulders, his knuckles brushing the silky flesh beneath her jaw as he adjusted the collar.

She stilled, something flashed in the depth of her eyes. Fear? Anxiety? It was there and gone too quickly for him to read.

"Thanks. I've never been so cold in my life. I guess that's another thing sho—" Her voice trailed off, her eyes widening as she caught sight of his side holster. "That's a gun."

"Right."

"You're carrying a weapon."

"Right."

"But…why?"

"I'm in the security business. I protect people and property."

"You're a bodyguard?"

"A security contractor."

"Which is the same as a bodyguard."

"If you want."

"What I want is to go back to last night and insist that Maureen spend it at my place."

"It would be nice if life had a do-over button, Shelby Ann, but it doesn't."

"I know. I just wish that I'd had a chance to save her." She swayed, her face colorless. He slid an arm around her waist, motioning to the EMT who was making his way toward them.

"Ma'am, why don't you sit down and let me have a look at your head?"

"I'm all right."

"You're bleeding, and you may have a concussion." The EMT used gloved fingers to probe Shelby's wound, and she stiffened.

"Ow!"

"Looks like you're going to need a few stitches. The doctor may want to do a CAT scan to rule out any fractures or brain bleeds. Let's get you transported to the hospital and see what's what."

"I really don't need to go to the hospital," Shelby protested.

"You really do," Ryder responded, urging her onto a stretcher that had been wheeled over by two other EMTs.

"But—"

"Just relax, ma'am, and let us do all the work." They rolled her away as she continued to protest.

Ryder figured he'd have a chat with the fire marshal and then find a place to buy some coffee, eat one of the protein bars that he kept in his glove compartment and get on with his day.

He scanned the mass of people fighting the blaze,

searching for the one who might be in charge. A dog
yapped from the bushes at the edge of the yard, but
he ignored it, focusing on the task, determined to
follow through on his plan.

"Wait! Stop!" Shelby's cry sent adrenaline pump-
ing through him, and he turned.

She hung over the side of the stretcher as she
whistled and called to something. If she leaned any
farther, she'd fall on her head. The EMTs seemed
helpless to stop her.

Ryder was not.

He covered the ground between them quickly,
grabbing her arm and hauling her up. "Are you nuts?
You're going to break your neck!"

"That's Mazy. I'm sure of it." She pointed to the
edge of the yard.

"Mazy who?"

"Mazy. Maureen's dog. She's probably scared to
death. Come here, Mazy. Here, girl," she called,
leaning over the side of the stretcher again.

"Cut it out before you kill yourself!" He grabbed
her arm again. Hauled her up again.

"But—"

"*I'll* go look for the dog. You stay put." Disgusted,
he tramped across the yard, following the sound of
yapping dog until he found a little white puffball
cowering in the bushes. It looked more like a piece
of fluff than a dog, but he picked it up anyway, ignoring its rumbling growl.

"This her?" He held the puffball out for Shelby to see, and she teared up.

"Yes. Poor thing. She must be so scared and confused."

"I'll take her to the shelter. She'll get good—"

"No! The other dogs will eat her alive."

She had a point. To a bigger dog, Mazy would probably look like a tasty morsel. "I can leave her here. Maybe Maureen had family or friends who will come and get her."

"You can't leave her here. She'll be—"

"Scared and confused?"

"Yes." She offered a half smile. "Listen, I hate to ask, but could you bring her to the hospital? I'll have someone meet us there and bring her to my place. That way, she won't run off while she's waiting for rescue."

Bring the dog to the hospital?

He frowned at the little beast, and he was pretty sure it frowned back, but Shelby was waiting, her eyes big and dark with concern, and *no* refused to make its way past his lips.

"Okay, but if she chews the upholstery in my truck, she's toast."

"Mazy has good manners. She'll behave." Shelby smiled the same sweet smile she greeted him with every time he walked into her bakery, and his pulse jumped, his blood warming.

He'd dated plenty of beautiful women during his time in the navy. After his injury and recovery, he'd been more selective, dating just a few women before he'd found Danielle. Gorgeous, driven and strong in her faith, she'd been the kind of woman he'd thought he could make a good life with, but after two years of dating, the relationship had felt hollow, Danielle's clawing, grasping need to get ahead putting a wedge between them.

He'd wanted a cozy home in the suburbs of New York City, a few kids, maybe a dog. She'd wanted a high-rise apartment in Manhattan, no kids, no pets. Nothing but work and money.

In the end, they hadn't found a way to make their goals mesh.

When he'd broken up with her, he hadn't bothered looking for another relationship. Ryder had had plenty of opportunity to find The One. But he hadn't, and he figured she wasn't out there.

But Shelby appealed to him, everything about her soft and warm and inviting. No matter how much he'd tried to ignore her, he couldn't. Four months of visiting her bakery, and he was no closer to understanding why.

She was pretty, sure, but that wasn't it.

When he looked into her eyes, it was like looking into her soul, and Ryder wanted to keep on looking.

He wasn't sure what to think about that.

Wasn't sure if he should think anything about it.

He'd come to Spokane to open another branch of his company, Personal Securities Incorporated. One year, that's what he'd planned to devote to setting things up. In eight months, he'd be going home to New York City. He didn't have time to get involved in a relationship, and he wasn't sure he would have wanted to if he did have the time.

But he couldn't seem to stay away from Shelby and her quaint bakery and easy smile.

He frowned, the dog whining and wiggling as the sirens blared and the ambulance sped away.

THREE

No way was Shelby *ever* going to let Dr. Jarrod Estes sew her up. She'd dated the man for about two minutes after she'd found Andrew and Stephanie kissing outside of Andrew's apartment building. One date with the most sought-after bachelor at Grace Christian Church, because Shelby had wanted to feel as if she wasn't the biggest loser on the planet. One date had been plenty. Jarrod had spent more time checking his text messages than talking to her, and Shelby had decided there and then that she was done with the dating scene.

Done.

Finished.

No more men.

Ever.

She'd made some lame excuse about leaving an oven on at the bakery and excused herself halfway through the entrée. Now the man she'd ditched on their first date was coming at her with a needle.

"Really, Jarrod, I don't think stitches are necessary." She eased off the exam table, her bare toes curling against cold tile, the acrid scent of smoke wafting from her hair.

Smoke from the explosions and fire that had killed Maureen.

Tears clogged her throat, but she'd already cried so much that her eyes were hot and dry.

"Shelby, I know you've had a tough morning, and I know you're anxious to get out of here and take some time to grieve, but you do need stitches." Jarrod dropped the needle back on the tray, glanced at his watch and sighed. "Tell you what, why don't I call Dottie and have her come to hold your hand?"

"Do *not* call Dottie." That was the last thing Shelby needed.

"How about one of your friends, then? Someone from church? Jasmine or Faith?" He leaned forward in his chair, a hint of impatience in his tone.

"I wouldn't want them to drive all the way here. Besides, I'm opting out of the stitches. I'm sure my head will heal just fine."

"It's going to scar," he warned.

"I can think of worse things." She scooped up her clothes and the jacket Ryder had thrown over her shoulders. Since Jarrod didn't seem keen on leaving the room, she'd find a restroom and change there. Sure, Ryder had said he'd bring Mazy to the hospital, but Shelby had seen the look in his eyes, and she figured he was about as likely to follow through as she was to let Jarrod stitch her up. She hadn't even bothered calling someone to come get the dog.

The only good man is a dead husband with a good life-insurance policy.

Another one of Beulah's truisms. One Shelby's mother and sister wholeheartedly believed. Shelby had tried to believe something different. She'd opened herself up to love, tried to create what Beulah and her mother had insisted was impossible—forever with a man who loved her for who she was.

Tried twice times, actually.

Once in college.

Once with Andrew.

Both had been disastrous.

She didn't plan to try again.

"Thanks for everything, Jarrod. See you at church Sunday." She yanked the door open, colliding with a rock-hard chest.

"What's the hurry, Shelby Ann?" Broad hands grabbed her waist as she caught her balance.

She knew the voice, the hands, the dark chocolate eyes that stared into hers.

Ryder.

Her heart jumped in acknowledgment, her body humming with an awareness she knew she shouldn't be feeling. "You came."

"I said I would," he responded, frowning slightly. "Is your friend around here somewhere? That dog and I aren't getting along, and I want her out of my car ASAP."

"Mazy gets along with everyone."

"She's not getting along with me. So, *where's your friend?*" He glanced at Jarrod, at the otherwise empty hospital room and then turned the full force of his gaze on Shelby again.

Yep. Dark chocolate eyes. Only they weren't sweet, they were hard and intense.

"I...didn't call anyone. I didn't think you'd actually come. You can just leave her..."

"Where?"

"Well..." Where *could* he leave her? "Just give me a minute to get changed and I'll get her." She tried to step past him, but he blocked her path.

"It's going to take more than a minute to get your head stitched up." He edged her backward.

"I'm not planning to have it stitched up."

"Shelby, will you please just let me get this done?" Jarrod asked, exasperated and not even trying to hide it.

"Fine." She walked back to the exam table, dropped her clothes and the coat on the chair beside it.

"Don't worry. You're going to feel this first stick, and then you won't feel a thing." Jarrod leaned toward her, the needle pointed straight at her face, and she felt every bit of blood drain from her head.

"You're not going to faint, are you?" Ryder put a hand on her shoulder.

"That would be preferable to the alternative."

"Which would be?"

"Staying conscious for the entire horrifying procedure."

Ryder laughed, the sound rusty and gruff. "It's not that bad, is it?"

"I guess that depends on which side of the needle you're on." Shelby winced as Jarrod shot her with the anesthetic.

"That's the worst of it, Shelby. Let's give it a minute to take effect. So—" Jarrod turned his attention to Ryder "—were you at Maureen's, too?"

"Yes." Ryder didn't offer more than that, and Shelby wondered if Jarrod would take the hint and stop asking questions.

He didn't.

"You work at the bakery with Shelby?"

"Why would you say that?" Ryder asked, and Jarrod frowned.

"Shelby said she was making a delivery when Maureen's house exploded."

"Shelby was making a delivery."

"And you were with her?"

"Is there a reason you want to know, Doctor?" Ryder asked as Jarrod lifted a needle and bent close to Shelby's head.

"Just curious. I was shocked to hear about the explosion and Maureen's death. I'm just trying to figure out how everything went down." Jarrod had the good grace to flush, his neck and cheeks going deep red.

"That's the job of the police and fire marshal. It may take a while for them to figure it out. The house is pretty much rubble. I'm not sure how easy it will be to piece together what happened."

"Did they find Maureen's...Maureen?" Shelby asked, and Ryder nodded.

"I'm afraid so."

"Poor Maureen." The tears Shelby had thought were completely dried up began again, slipping down her cheeks as Jarrod worked.

"If it makes you feel any better, she didn't suffer. If the initial explosion didn't kill her, the smoke overcame her so quickly, she didn't have time to be scared," Ryder offered, patting her back as Jarrod continued his slow, methodical stitching.

"Dead is dead. She should be flying to New York right now, celebrating with her friends. Not lying in a morgue," Shelby said, taking a tissue Ryder shoved toward her.

"She's celebrating in a different way." Jarrod's easy platitude did more to irritate Shelby than it did to comfort her. She knew Maureen was a Christian, but that didn't make her death any less tragic.

"I think, if given the choice, she'd rather be on the plane."

"Right," Jarrod conceded, stepping back. "Okay, you're all set. I'm going to send a nurse in with aftercare instructions. See your personal physician tomorrow. The stitches will need to come out in ten days."

"Thanks." She stood on wobbling legs, grabbing the closest thing to her, which just happened to be Ryder's arm. She jerked back, the spark of electricity that shot through her palm an unwelcome surprise.

What was it about the man that made her heart race every time she looked in his eyes? That made heat shoot through her when she touched his arm?

It certainly wasn't his winning smile or charming personality. The guy looked like a carved statue of a Roman centurion, all hard angles and cold calculation.

"I need to get changed," she mumbled, turning away.

"I'll be right outside." He stepped into the hall and closed the door.

Alone, Shelby dressed quickly, pulling on her white polo shirt and the faded jeans that were just a little looser than they'd been when she'd broken up with Andrew. Ten pounds lost so she could fit into a fancy black dress. It all seemed futile now, the worry, the wondering if she'd look beautiful enough to make Andrew regret his lying, cheating ways, a waste of time.

She sighed as she tied her lilac apron. Just Desserts' insignia emblazoned on the front, it was the only uniform she required for people working at the bakery. It was Beulah's favorite color and a nod to the grandmother who'd provided the funds to open the shop. Today, Shelby's normally immaculate apron was soot marred and grass stained, splotches of blood mixing with the green-and-black mess, a modern painting that spoke of chaos and tragedy. She'd have to throw it away. No way would she ever get the stains out, and she couldn't imagine wearing it without crying.

Someone knocked on the door, and she pulled it open, expecting Ryder to be standing impatiently on the other side.

"Hold your horses, big guy. I'm almost…" Her voice trailed off as she looked into the face of a stocky, middle-aged man.

"Sorry. I thought you were someone else." She glanced down the hall, surprised at how disappointed she was to see it empty.

"Mr. Malone is speaking with the sheriff. I'm sure he'll be back shortly. I'm Fire Chief Timothy Saddles, Spokane County Fire Marshal. How are you feeling?"

"Okay. All things considered."

"It's been a rough morning. I'm sorry to say your friend lost her life in the fire."

"Ryder…Mr. Malone told me you'd found her remains."

"We did. They've been sent to the medical examiner and will be released to the family once he's finished."

Medical examiner? That made Maureen's death sound less like an accident and more like...

Murder?

Shelby's pulse jumped, her thoughts spinning back to those moments before she'd rung Maureen's doorbell, back to the man with the sunglasses jogging away from Maureen's street.

"Is that common procedure? I thought the medical examiner only made rulings on suspicious deaths."

"Not really, ma'am. His job is to determine cause of death when an examination by a physician can't determine it. In this case, we're assuming the explosion killed the deceased, but assumptions don't make for good investigations. Now, if you don't mind, I'd like to ask you a few questions."

"Go ahead."

"Mr. Malone said you were making a delivery to the deceased's—"

"Maureen."

"Pardon?"

"The *deceased* was Maureen. A bestselling author, a mother, a good friend. I was making a delivery to her place because it was her birthday, and she had invited a dozen friends to go on a shopping trip to New York City. They were going to meet at her house, have some breakfast and then take a limo to the airport."

"My apologies if I sounded callous, Ms. Simons. What time did you arrive at Maureen's house?"

"At 5:25. Five minutes later than she had asked me to be there."

"Did you notice anything out of the ordinary? Anything different about the house?"

"There was a guy jogging down South Hill as I was heading up it. I saw him come off her street."

"Plenty of people jog on South Hill," Chief Saddles said as he jotted something in a small notebook.

"I know, but he was wearing sunglasses and gloves. It struck me as…odd."

"Did you get a good look at his face?"

"He was Caucasian. Medium complexion. Maybe five-ten. I didn't see his hair. It was covered by a hood."

"It was a chilly morning. A hood and jacket wouldn't be out of the ordinary. Gloves, either, for that matter. We'll ask around, though. Maybe he lives in one of the houses on 21st."

Maybe.

But Shelby couldn't help shuddering as she remembered the way he'd turned, taken a step toward her.

"Do you know what caused the explosion?" she asked, trying to refocus her thoughts and get ahold of her wild imagination. He *hadn't* followed her, *hadn't* tried to harm her, hadn't done anything except jog by and look, then turn and look again.

As if he were memorizing her features.

Trying to make sure he'd recognize her if he saw her again.

"A gas leak in the heater. It looks like the heating unit cracked, gas escaped. One spark of electricity from old wiring and the whole place went up."

"A spark? Like from someone ringing the doorbell?" Shelby asked, cold with the thought. Had *she* killed her friend?

"It's possible. Either that, or Maureen turned on a light—"

"All the lights were off. The only electricity was from me ringing the doorbell twice. It's my fault, isn't it? I killed her." She dropped into a chair, her stomach sick, those stupid tears back again.

"Of course you didn't, ma'am." The chief patted her arm awkwardly, and Shelby almost felt sorry for him.

"Everything okay in here?" Ryder stepped into the room, his height and oversize muscles dwarfing the average-size fire chief, his dark gaze on Shelby.

"You're crying again." He stated the obvious, and she frowned, irritated with him, with herself and with the fire chief, who hovered uneasily a few feet away.

"Because I just realized I killed my friend."

"Ma'am, your friend may very well have been dead before the gas was ignited. The amount of gas it took to cause such a catastrophic explosion was enough to asphyxiate her while she slept."

"That really doesn't make me feel any better, Chief." But she stood anyway, refusing to meet

Ryder's eyes as she shoved his jacket into his arms. "I really need to get to work. Are we done here?"

"Yes. Just give me your contact information, and I'll call if I have any more questions."

Shelby spouted off her home address and her cell-phone number, and gave the chief the bakery's address for good measure.

"Will you call me once you have news from the medical examiner?" she asked.

"Of course. You'll probably hear from me in a day or two. If not, give me a call." He handed her a business card, and she shoved it in her apron pocket.

His findings wouldn't change the fact that Maureen was dead, but they might ease some of the guilt Shelby was suddenly feeling.

She'd felt the same way when Beulah had died alone in a hospital in Beverly Hills while Shelby sat in an airport in Seattle waiting for her connecting flight. She'd been trying to get to her grandmother after receiving a late-night call from the nursing home saying Beulah had had a heart attack, but all the trying in the world hadn't put her where she needed to be when she needed to be there.

And all the crying in the world couldn't undo what had happened at Maureen's house, because crying over spilled milk never got the mess cleaned up.

That's what Beulah would have said, and Shelby knew it was true. When Dottie had shown up on her doorstep, homeless because she'd been kicked out of Beulah's Beverly Hills rental property, Shelby had let her live in her spare room, offered her a job at the bakery, made her feel like family, because she'd known it was what Beulah would have wanted. Shelby hadn't been able to be at her grandmother's side when she'd died, but she *had* carried on the legacy of kindness and compassion that Beulah had shown to the people in her life.

She might not be able to bring Maureen back to life, but Shelby could press the fire marshal and the police to find the reason for Maureen's death. It's what Maureen would want. Complete disclosure. Absolute truth. Just like she always wrote in her true-crime books.

The fire chief left the room, his shoulders stooped, his hair mussed. He'd probably been sleeping when he'd been called out to Maureen's place. Shelby had a feeling he wouldn't be sleeping much in the next few days.

"Come on. Let's get out of here." Ryder cupped her elbow, led her through the quiet hospital corridor. Shelby didn't bother telling him she needed to wait for aftercare instructions, because she didn't want to wait. She wanted to go to the bakery, lose herself in the process of creating cakes and cookies and pastries.

"Thanks again for bringing Mazy."

"I probably should say it wasn't a problem."

"But it was?"

"She chewed a hole in my car's upholstery, so yeah, it was."

"I'll pay you for the damage."

"You weren't the one who chewed the hole," he growled, but Shelby thought there might be a glimmer of amusement in his eyes.

"No, but I did ask you to give her a ride here."

"You asked. I said yes. I'm as culpable as you."

"I can pay for half of the repair cost, then."

"No need, but for future reference, when I say I'm going to do something, I follow through. I expect other people to do the same."

"I'll keep that in mind." Not that she thought that she'd have any reason to.

Dating was out of the question. Men were off-limits.

If she wanted to remember that, she needed to stay far away from guys like Ryder.

She *would* stay far away from him. As soon as she got Mazy out of his car.

They stepped outside into the bright morning sunlight, the vivid blue sky and fluffy white clouds too beautiful for the ugliness of the day. Maureen would have been so pleased with the weather, the clear skies, everything about her fiftieth birthday. Mazy barked hysterically as Ryder led Shelby to his Hummer, and Shelby was sure she must know that her owner was dead.

Poor little dog.

"Be careful. She's a menace," Ryder warned as he opened the door.

"Hey, girl." Shelby pulled Mazy into her arms, doing her best not to cry again. Unlike her mother and sister, who always looked beautiful when they cried, Shelby looked like a mess and felt even worse when the tears flowed. Blotchy skin, bright red nose, raging headache. She was heading for all three.

"Thanks again, Ryder. I'll make sure to tell Dottie to keep you supplied with doughnuts and coffee when I'm not at the bakery." She started to walk away, but Ryder snagged her hand, his palm rough and callused and way too wonderful.

"You're not planning on walking to the bakery," he said, his forehead creased, fine lines fanning out from his eyes. He had long, golden eyelashes and dark gold hair, and he really did look like a Roman statue come to life. Sleek, hard muscles and strong lines. Beautiful in a very masculine way.

"Yes, I am. It's only two miles from here."

"Maybe I should rephrase that. You're not *going* to walk to the bakery."

"Of course I am. I make deliveries here all the time, and when the weather is nice and the deliveries are small enough, I walk. It'll take me a half hour, tops."

"Not if you pass out from your head injury on the way there."

"I haven't passed out yet. There's no reason to think I will."

"Listen, Shelby Ann." Ryder sighed, obviously holding on to his patience with difficulty. "I was supposed to be at work a half hour ago. I have a meeting in an hour. I'd really like to be there. If I drive you to the bakery, I'll make it. If I follow you to the bakery to make sure you arrive safely, I won't. So, get in the Hummer and let's get going."

"You don't have to follow me."

"Yeah. I do. So *get in*." He lifted her off her feet, plopping her onto the passenger seat with ease.

"Hey!"

"Move your legs," he ordered, nearly closing the door on her when she didn't move fast enough.

"This is kidnapping," she sputtered as he climbed in.

"If I were going to kidnap you, I'd make sure the dog wasn't with you when I did it. One hole in the upholstery is enough." His bland reply almost made Shelby smile.

"You're a Neanderthal, you know that, Ryder?" she asked without heat as she fastened her seat belt. His hands had been on her waist, and she could still feel the imprint of his thumbs on her belly. Her soft haven't-done-a-sit-up-in-ten-years belly.

She cracked open the window, letting crisp morning air cool her flushed cheeks.

"A Neanderthal, huh?" Ryder smiled as he drove

through the parking lot, and Shelby's pulse had the nerve to jump in response.

"If the shoe fits…"

"Did they wear shoes back then?"

"They might have. Of course, even if they didn't, a guy who picks a woman up and throws her in his car is still…" She lost her train of thought; a man at the corner of the hospital parking lot caught her attention.

Dark glasses that glinted in the light. Hood pulled over his hair.

Medium height.

Medium build.

As she watched, he pulled down the glasses, stared straight into her eyes, his gaze hollow and icy-blue.

"That's him," she shouted, as he turned and walked around the corner.

"Who?" Ryder braked, leaning past her and looking in the direction she pointed.

"The guy I saw this morning running from 21st Street. He's heading down Main Street."

"Stay in the car. I'll go see what he has to say."

He was out of the Hummer before Shelby could respond, moving quickly, bypassing a few pedestrians as he jogged around the corner and out of sight.

Going to find the guy with the icy-blue eyes.

Shelby shuddered, smoothing Mazy's silky head. "He'll be fine, right, girl?"

The dog whined, but it wasn't the answer Shelby wanted.

She wanted to know absolutely for sure that Ryder wasn't going to run into a trap and be brought down by the strange guy with the sunglasses.

Ten minutes passed. Then another ten.

Ryder had a meeting to get to, and Shelby had a desperate need to know he was okay.

She set Mazy on the seat.

"Stay here and don't chew anything." She tossed the command out as she opened the door and jumped out. The quick movement was a mistake. Her head spun, and she grabbed the door, steadying herself as she took deep gulps of air.

"I thought I told you to stay in the Hummer," Ryder snapped, and Shelby jumped, her heart racing double-time as she met his dark eyes.

"I was worried about you."

"You should have been worried about *you*. You're pale as paper. Sit down before you fall down." His tone was gruff, his hands gentle as he helped her back into the SUV.

"Did you find him?"

"No. That doesn't mean he wasn't there. There are plenty of places to hide around here, that's for sure, and if he took off his hood and sunglasses, I could easily have looked right at him and not known it." He glanced around the parking lot, his jacket pulled back just enough to show the edge of his shoulder holster.

A security contractor, that's what he'd called himself. He looked like one. Tough and determined and very confident.

"I know it was him, Ryder. He was waiting for me." She shuddered, and Ryder patted her knee. Heat radiated up her leg and settled deep in her belly. She ignored it. Ignored the flush that raced across her cheeks.

"Just because he's the same guy you saw this morning doesn't mean he was waiting for you. He might be indigent. It's possible he spent the night at Manito Park and then came this way for something to eat."

True. The park was just a few blocks away from Maureen's, and the Union Gospel Mission was around the corner from the hospital. It all made perfect sense, but Shelby's shivering fear wouldn't leave.

"Maybe you're right."

"I'm going to call hospital security. See if they can pull up external security-camera footage for me. I want to get a good look at this guy." He pulled out of the parking lot, the Hummer's engine purring as he drove toward the bakery.

Shelby's unsettled stomach churned and grumbled as Ryder talked to a hospital security officer on his hands-free phone, his tone brusque.

She closed her eyes. The day had started horribly, but it didn't have to continue that way. She'd go to the bakery, work for a few hours, then take

Mazy to her apartment, get her set up there. Maybe she'd forget that she'd rung the doorbell and sealed Maureen's fate.

Maybe.

But Shelby doubted it.

A lone tear slid down her cheek, and she let it fall, because her friend was dead, because Shelby might have killed her and because there was absolutely nothing she could do to change any of it.

FOUR

Shelby seemed to be sleeping as Ryder parked in front of Just Desserts. Pale and drawn, a large bandage on her temple, she looked very young and very vulnerable. That worried him. *She* worried him. Despite what he'd told her, Ryder didn't believe in coincidence, and he didn't believe that the guy she'd seen was some random homeless person. He'd been there for Shelby. Ryder's gut told him that, and he always listened to his gut.

He'd called the hospital security team and spoken to the head of security, but the thirty-second conversation had revealed little. They'd check their surveillance footage and said they'd report anything suspicious, but Ryder doubted a guy standing on the street corner would be viewed as that.

He frowned, eyeing the news vans parked in the bakery's parking lot. Obviously, news of the fire, Maureen's death and Shelby's involvement had spread.

"Are we at the bakery?" Shelby opened her eyes and blinked groggily. Dark curls slid across her forehead and cheeks. Wild and silky-looking, they begged to be touched.

"I thought you were sleeping."

"It takes me longer than five minutes to fall asleep. It didn't sound as if your conversation with hospital security went well." She scooped Mazy into her arms and got out of the Hummer. Ryder followed, falling into step beside her as she made her way across the crowded parking lot.

"They're being as helpful as they can. I'll call the sheriff later. He may be interested in viewing the footage."

"Maybe, but you're probably right. The guy was hanging around waiting for the mission to open." She smiled as she walked into the bakery, the scent of vanilla and chocolate and rich yeast dough stroking Ryder's senses almost as completely as Shelby did.

He frowned, not comfortable with the thought.

"Wow. This is…insane," Shelby whispered, clutching his arm for a moment and releasing it just as quickly.

She was right.

The bakery was jam-packed.

"I'll take care of it," he responded, shoving his way through the crowd.

A team of reporters stood near the counter, shouting questions above the quiet roar of ordering patrons and busybody visitors. Shelby's harried young employees scurried from person to person, answering questions, ringing up orders.

Ryder eased his way through the crowd, sidling up next to the loudest of three news crews.

"Leave," he said quietly, and the anchorwoman frowned.

"Excuse me?" she asked as if she weren't sure she'd heard him right.

"Ms. Simons won't be answering any questions today. If you're interested in an interview, you'll have to call ahead of time and set up an appointment."

"But—"

"You've been asked to leave, and now you're trespassing. I suggest you take my advice and go before I call the police." He left her openmouthed and unhappy, and moved on to the next crew.

Ten minutes later, the crowd had thinned to a manageable number, air circulated through the small bakery once again, the harried young girl and her tattooed male counterpart behind the counter were working in harmony once again.

Mission accomplished.

He turned to call Shelby over, but she'd disappeared. He could hear her voice drifting from the kitchen, and he knew she was safe.

He could leave, go to his meeting and get on with his day. Only he wasn't sure he should leave before he made sure Shelby was okay.

As a matter of fact, he was certain he shouldn't.

He walked to the counter, smiled at the blonde teenager. "Is Shelby in the back?"

"Yes, I think so. I mean, she could have walked out the back door, but she never does that." She glanced over her shoulder, and Ryder took the opportunity to step around the counter.

"Sir! You can't come back here."

"I just did." He smiled again and walked into the kitchen.

"What are you doing back here? Git!" A blue-haired lady came at him with a broom, and Ryder sidestepped her swing.

Dottie. The bane of his existence. Refusing to serve him coffee and doughnuts had been bad enough. Now she was trying to beat him with a broom. He grabbed it before she could swing again, slipping it out of her hands.

"Where's Shelby?"

"Why should I tell you?"

"Dottie! There's no need to be rude." Shelby stepped out of a walk-in pantry, a huge bag of flour clutched in her hands.

"That thing is as big as you are. You should have gotten that tattooed employee of yours to carry it." Ryder took it from her hands, and she shrugged.

"I'm stronger than he is. Dottie, why don't you go up front and help? They're swamped up there."

"Are you trying to get rid of me?"

"Yes."

"Well, then! I guess I'll go." Dottie huffed away.

"Sorry about that. Dottie has…issues." Shelby opened the sack of flour and measured several cups into a standing mixer.

"Apparently I'm one of them."

"*Everyone* is one of them."

"Yet you employ her."

"I inherited her from my grandmother. They were good friends. When Beulah passed away, I got Dottie." She smiled, finally looking into his eyes. "I thought you'd left. You have that meeting to get to, remember?"

"I wanted to make sure you were okay."

"Aside from a raging headache, I'm fine."

"You need to go home, Shelby. That was a pretty serious head injury you sustained."

"It's not the head injury that's giving me a headache. It's all the tears. I always get headaches when I cry." She poured milk into the mixer, added eggs and soft butter and sugar, her hands pretty and efficient. He'd like to take her to the gun range. Show her how to handle a semiautomatic. He had a feeling she'd be a good shot.

"Yeah? Then I'll have to be sure to never make you cry."

"Why would you? You come in for doughnuts and coffee every day. That's money in my pocket. Which makes me very happy." She offered a tight smile and turned her attention to the bowl. Obviously, he'd hit a nerve.

"Is that doughnut batter? Because I never did get my breakfast," he said.

"No. It's sweet bread. I'm going to put it in the fridge to proof, and then I'm going home. I need to get Mazy settled, and I need to settle a little, too. It's been a rough morning." She covered the bowl with a damp cloth, slid it onto a rolling rack with ten other bowls and pushed everything into a walk-in refrigerator.

"Where's the dog? I'll get her for you and walk you to your car."

"Ryder, I appreciate your help, but I don't need it anymore." She brushed flour from her apron, and he brushed it from her cheek, his fingers grazing silky flesh.

She stilled.

"Ryder…"

"You had flour on your cheek."

"Oh. Okay." She rubbed the spot he'd touched, not meeting his eyes.

"So, where's the dog?"

"Dottie tied her up out back," she responded and then pressed her lips together. "You tricked that out of me."

"No trick, Shelby Ann. You're exhausted and traumatized. Whether you want to admit it or not, you need a little help."

She sighed. "Fine. Go get Mazy. I'll meet you out front. My car is—"

"The big pink Cadillac."

"How did you know?"

"It's the only car that's here every time you are."

"Right. Okay. I'll meet you out there in a couple of minutes. I just need to give my crew some instructions." She hurried away. Ran, actually.

He walked out the back exit, freed the ungrateful Mazy and carried her to Shelby's car. He waited there, holding the struggling dog as tightly as he could without squashing her. Ten minutes passed. Fifteen. Twenty. He called work, rescheduled the meeting for later in the afternoon, tapped his fingers on the Caddie's hood.

Where was she?

Probably mixing another batch of sweet bread or keeping Dottie from attacking a patron. What she needed to be doing was resting. He shoved Mazy into the Hummer and walked into the bakery.

Shelby stood at one of the small booths, talking to an elderly couple, her blue eyes widening with surprise as she met his gaze.

"Time to go." He took her arm, tugging her away.

"But I was—"

"Going home to take a nap, remember?"

"I know, but Dottie, Zane and Rae—"

"Can handle things just fine." He led her outside, grabbing Mazy from the back of his Hummer and waiting while Shelby climbed into the Cadillac.

"Come on, Old Blue. Give me a break this time

and start, okay?" she muttered as she turned the key in the ignition.

"I hate to break the news to you, Shelby. But your car is pink, not blue." He leaned in the open door and set Mazy in Shelby's lap, caught a whiff of vanilla and berry, his muscles tightening in response.

"I know. Terrible, isn't it? Beulah left it to me in her will with specific instructions to keep it pink. If I had my way, though, she'd be blue."

"She?"

"Of course. She's not just a car. Blue is an old lady with history. She's been through a lot, but she's still nice to have around. Most of the time."

"Like Dottie?"

"Exactly. Thanks again for all your help this morning. I don't know what I would have done if you hadn't been at Maureen's place." Her eyes grew moist with tears at the mention of her friend, but she didn't let them fall. Instead, she closed the door, offered a quick wave and drove away.

He watched until the pink Cadillac disappeared from view, something in him soft for Shelby, soft for her easy smile and compassionate nature. To keep a woman like Dottie around, to drive an old pink car in memory of a woman who'd been gone for years, to run a successful bakery with a ragtag group of teens and a crotchety old woman behind the counter took a special kind of person.

Shelby was definitely that.

Ryder had been attracted to women before.

He'd even thought he might love a few of them, but none of them had touched his heart so easily, so completely as Shelby seemed to.

He rubbed the knotted muscles in his thigh before he climbed into the Hummer. He needed to work the pain out, run until the muscles heated and loosened, but he had a meeting to attend, a client to impress. He had a company to run and his own set of problems to deal with. The last thing he needed or wanted was to be pulled into someone else's life or drama.

But with Shelby, he wasn't sure he'd have to be pulled.

With Shelby, he had a feeling he'd end up fighting his way into her life, and he had a feeling it would be worth it.

Drama and all.

He pulled away from Just Desserts, his mind humming with the million things he had to do before the day ended. Plenty to keep him occupied, but Shelby's sweet smile and berry-and-vanilla scent lingered just below the surface of his thoughts, reminding him of cool summer breezes and sparkling blue waters.

Laughter and joy and home.

All the things he'd craved most when he'd been in the arid Afghanistan countryside. Everything he'd longed for when he'd been lying in a hospital bed, listening while doctors told him he'd never walk again.

Six years ago, God had given Ryder a second chance at life, and Ryder had promised to live better and love more. He'd followed through on that, honoring his fallen comrades by building a successful security business and setting up scholarship funds for their children.

But the one thing he'd longed for most since those dark, pain-filled days had remained out of reach.

Family.

Not just his parents and siblings, but that deeper, all-consuming connection built between husband and wife and children. He'd seen its power as wives and children crowded around the beds of his surviving team members, felt it in the air as he visited the widows of those he'd served with, and he'd wanted it in a way that he never had before the explosion in Afghanistan.

Wanted it.

Sought it.

Thought he might have found it in Danielle. After they'd broken up, he'd decided that family wasn't part of God's plan for his life. Maybe he'd been right, but Ryder wasn't the kind who turned away from an opportunity, and when he looked at Shelby, that's what he saw.

An opportunity.

To look one more time for forever.

Maybe he'd find it.

Maybe he wouldn't.

Either way, he had a feeling he was in for a bumpy ride.

FIVE

"Start, you stupid lump of metal. Start!" Shelby turned the key in the ignition and listened to Blue's engine sputter and die for the tenth time.

"Perfect," she muttered, leaning her forehead against the steering wheel, her head throbbing from a sleepless night and a million tears. She should have stayed in bed. She'd *planned* to stay in bed, but Dottie had called to say the doughnut fryer was acting up and that she needed Shelby to fix it.

That had been nearly an hour ago, and Shelby was still sitting in the driveway of her two-story Tudor, trying to start the Cadillac as dawn stretched gold fingers across the horizon.

She'd have to walk.

There were no two ways about it.

Walk the three miles to the bakery and hope the guy who'd haunted her dreams wasn't waiting around a corner or hiding in a dark alley.

She frowned, rubbing the bridge of her nose and praying that if she gave Old Blue one last shot, she'd start.

But nothing had been easy lately.

Not breaking up with Andrew, not facing the pitying looks of her friends and the I-told-you-so's of her family. Not running the bakery with Dottie and four high-school dropouts who'd needed a place to work.

Not answering dozens of phone calls about Maureen's death.

Not trying to sleep when Maureen's dog howled and cried for her owner.

Nothing had been easy lately.

So, *of course,* Old Blue wouldn't start.

She turned the key again and again and again, tears streaming down her face and probably smearing the makeup she'd applied to try to hide the fact that she'd spent most of the night crying.

She didn't care.

Because the stupid car would *not* start, and she was too afraid to walk, and right at that very moment her life stunk.

The Cadillac door opened, and she screamed, slapping at a hand that reached in to snatch the keys, her pulse racing with terror, the metallic taste of fear on her tongue as she tried desperately to escape through the other door.

Someone snagged her belt loop, easily pulling her back.

"You need to be more careful with your key, Shelby Ann. You break it in the ignition, and then where will you be?" Ryder's deep voice poured over her, thick and rich as melted chocolate, and Shelby collapsed onto the seat, all the strength seeping out of her.

"What are you doing here?" she asked, wiping at her cheeks as she straightened.

"Dottie was worried when you didn't show at the bakery. She wouldn't—"

"Let you buy your doughnuts and coffee until you came and checked on me?"

"Exactly. Looks like you're having car trouble again. Need some help?" He leaned in, sweat trickling down his brow, his breath coming hard and steady, his blond hair dark with moisture. Had he been running? She glanced around. No Hummer. That explained why she hadn't heard him arrive.

"Blue is being fickle lately, but I'll get her started. Go on back to the bakery. I'll meet you there."

"Actually, I was hoping to catch a ride back with you. I did a five-mile run to the bakery and a three-mile run here. My leg is protesting." He rubbed the muscle of his thigh and grimaced.

"You strained it?"

"It's an old injury. It acts up once in a while. How about you let me give Old Blue a try? Maybe we'll both make it back to the bakery before Dottie sends out a search party." He slid into the car before Shelby could protest, nudging her out of the way and sliding the key into Blue's ignition.

"She's not going to start," Shelby said as he turned the key.

So, of course, Blue started.

"There. Piece of cake. Buckle up, and let's get out of here."

"I can drive."

"I thought all the black stuff around your eyes might make it difficult to see the road."

Black stuff?

Shelby pulled her compact out of the Gucci purse her sister had given her for Christmas and looked in the mirror.

Mascara ran from both eyes. Shelby grabbed tissue from the glove compartment, dabbing at the mess.

"A gentleman wouldn't have mentioned how awful I look," she grumbled as Ryder pulled out of the driveway.

"Who said I was a gentleman?" he responded. "And who said you look awful?"

"I've got mascara running down my face. Of course I look awful."

"Actually, you look beautiful. Even with black tears running down your face."

"There's no need to flatter me to get doughnuts." She tried to keep her tone light, but she was still shaky from the surprise of seeing him, sweaty and gorgeous and too perfect for words, before she'd even had her first cup of coffee.

"Flattery implies an undeserved compliment. I'm not into that sort of thing."

"Then what sort of thing are you into?" she asked, and he shot her a look that curled her toes.

"Honesty."

"Oh. Well, that's good." She felt gauche and schoolgirlish, and she didn't like the feeling at all. She took a deep breath, steadied her thoughts and her thundering heart. He might look like Hercules, but he was a man, and she was done with men forever.

"I need to apologize for Dottie. She shouldn't have sent you out looking for me." Better. Much better.

"She should apologize for herself."

"She won't. The thing is, she means well, and the good news is, eventually, she'll get over her fixation with you—"

"Fixation?"

"She thinks I should be dating. She keeps trying to fix me up with customers. Last month, it was Mr. Hampton, the president of the seniors' birding society. He's eighty-nine."

"Ouch!"

"Exactly."

"I'm curious, Shelby Ann. What does all this have to do with you crying your eyes out?" He pulled into Just Desserts' crowded parking lot, found a spot and turned to face her, his dark eyes scanning her face as if he could read the truth there.

"Nothing. This place is busy for six o'clock in the morning. I'd better get in there and fix the doughnut machine." She opened the door, but he grabbed her hand, his touch light but so compelling she couldn't force herself to pull away.

"It's fixed. Dottie had me look at it before she sent me to find you."

"I still need to get in there."

"Is there any reason why you don't want to answer my question?"

"Is there a reason why you asked?"

"Because I'd be happy to take care of him if you need me to."

"There is no him." Not anymore.

"No?" He slid one of her curls between his fingers. "I think I might be glad about that, Shelby Ann."

"Ryder..."

"So, if you weren't crying about a man, you were crying about Maureen." He changed the subject, and she was relieved. She didn't want to think about what he'd meant, didn't want to *know* what he'd meant, because she really couldn't believe he'd meant anything.

A flirt, a player, that's what he had to be, but when she looked into his eyes, she was pretty sure he wasn't either of those things.

"Look," she said, "Maureen is dead. I feel like it's my fault, like maybe I could have saved her if I'd done something different. This stupid car never starts when I want it to, and my head is pounding, and I've got a whole day of work ahead of me.

That's why I was crying. Happy?" The words spilled out, and he shook his head.

"Not if you aren't. You couldn't have saved Maureen, Shelby Ann. No matter what you did. She was dead before the explosion."

"The fire marshal hasn't confirmed that yet." Though she'd called before she'd left the house and left a message reminding him to call as soon as he heard anything.

"Because he doesn't have a friend who works for the medical examiner. I do. I called this morning. The autopsy is almost complete. They're just waiting on toxicology reports before they release their findings."

"So, the gas asphyxiated her?"

"No. She was killed by blunt-force trauma to the head."

"What?"

"Someone murdered her, Shelby, and made it look like an accident. That's one of the reasons I was here before the bakery opened this morning. I wanted to let you know that you need to be very, very careful. If the guy you saw is responsible for Maureen's death, he might not be content to leave any loose ends."

Loose ends?

As in, Shelby?

She shivered, remembering his hollow, icy stare. "Thanks, Ryder. I'll be careful. Now, I guess, I'd better get inside and help Dottie handle this rush. Do you want a couple of doughnuts to go?"

"What I want is to know that you're going to be okay," he said quietly. She looked into his eyes again and was caught in his dark gaze.

"I'm always okay, Ryder. It's just part of who I am," she responded, but her voice shook, because he seemed to see beyond her cheerful facade, seemed to see so much more than anyone else ever had.

"I don't think so. I think you're always running around making sure everyone else is okay, and I don't think you spend five seconds worrying about whether or not you are. Come on. I'll walk you into the bakery." He got out of Old Blue, and she had no choice but to follow.

Because he was right.

She did have to make sure the people she cared about were okay.

The bakery teemed with people, its walls seeming to bow from the force of so many bodies, and Shelby hurried behind the counter, taking a customer's order, answering half a dozen questions about the fire and Maureen, and then moving on to the next guest.

Over and over again.

The same routine.

Serve, answer, serve, answer, her head pounding, her body sluggish, Ryder's words echoing through her mind.

Killed by blunt-force trauma to the head.

"You okay, boss?" Zane Thunderbird asked. At nineteen, Zane had lived through more than most people double his age. Kicked out of his stepfather's home when he was sixteen, he'd been homeless for nearly two years when he'd walked into Just Desserts, tattooed and pierced and offering to wash the bakery windows in exchange for food and coffee.

Shelby had given him a job instead, and now he was in college, studying to become a nurse. She couldn't be more proud, and the last thing she wanted to do was worry him. "Just a headache, Zane. You know how I get when I'm tired."

"Then go home and rest. We can handle the bakery for another day or two while you recover."

"Are you kidding? This place is hopping. We need all hands on deck."

"All *capable* hands, and yours aren't. Not today," Dottie cut in, her blue hair vibrating with the force of her words. "You get on out of here. Go home and sleep."

"You're the one who called me to come in, Dottie."

"To fix the fryer. It's fixed. So, go."

"Ms. Simons?" A tall, thin man cut in front of the line of customers and stepped to the counter, his dark hair receding from a broad forehead.

"If you're a reporter, she doesn't have time for an interview," Dottie growled, and the man pulled a wallet from his pocket, flashing a badge and ID.

"I'm Sheriff Lionel Jones with the Spokane

County Sheriff's Department. I have a few questions I'd like to ask if you have a minute."

"Sure." Shelby wiped her hands on her apron and stepped out from behind the counter, stopping short when she saw Ryder sitting in a booth near the front door. She'd been sure he was gone, but there he was, watching her with a dark, steady gaze.

"Would you like to do the interview here or down at the station?" the sheriff asked, and Shelby forced herself to look away from Ryder and focus on the conversation.

"Here is fine. I have a small office in the back, or we can sit in a booth."

"A booth is good. I wouldn't mind a cup of coffee and a blueberry muffin, if it wouldn't be too much trouble. It's been a long night." The sheriff smiled, his gaunt, solemn face transforming into something nearly handsome and much more approachable.

"Go ahead and have a seat. I'll bring you something." Shelby grabbed a muffin and a steaming cup of coffee and set them down in front of the sheriff, studiously ignoring Ryder as she slid into the booth behind him.

"So, what did you want to ask?" She brushed imaginary crumbs from the table, restless and anxious to get the interview over with. Though the morning crowd had thinned, she was sure the lunch rush would be hectic, and she needed to make sure the staff was prepared.

"Mind if I take notes?" The sheriff pulled out an iPad from its case, and Shelby shook her head.

"Not at all."

"Good. I'm sure you've heard that Maureen Lewis's death may not be an accident."

"Yes."

"We should know for sure tomorrow, but I'd like to ask you about her friends and family. Was she close to anyone in particular? Did she have a boyfriend? A love interest? Any enemies that you know of?"

"No love interest. No boyfriend. I think she broke up with the last guy she dated over two years ago."

"What about her family? Were they close?"

"She has an ex-husband, who lives in London, and a son, who lives in Chicago. She doesn't have any contact with her ex, and I don't think she and her son are...were very close."

"How about enemies?"

"I don't know. Maureen was a good friend, but she could be tough to get along with. She was demanding and expected things to be done her way. Not everyone appreciates that."

"How about her work? Did she ever complain about it? Did she receive threats from anyone she was interviewing or writing about?"

"Not recently. At least not that she mentioned. She started a new project last month, and she seemed really caught up in it."

"Do you know what she was working on?"

"A book about the Good Samaritan murders." The case had been all over the news four years ago when a nurse named Catherine Miller was convicted of murdering eleven patients at Good Samaritan Convalescent Center.

"I'll check into it. I have a report that you saw someone leaving 21st Street yesterday morning?"

"That's right." She gave a quick description, then explained that she'd seen the same man outside the hospital.

"That was reported, too. Another reason I wanted to stop by and talk to you. You're sure it was the same guy?"

"As sure as I can be."

"We've already canvassed Maureen's street. There's no one in any of the houses that will admit to being out jogging yesterday morning. I'm going to call the state police. They have a composite-sketch artist on staff. Hopefully, we can get her down here in the next day or two. Will you be able to come to the station to work up the sketch with her?"

"Sure."

"Good. I think that's it. At the moment, it doesn't seem like you're in imminent danger, but be careful."

"I will be."

"I'll give you a call if we turn up any more information. Have a good day, Ms. Simons." The sheriff finished his coffee and took his muffin as he left.

Seconds later, Ryder slid into the booth across from Shelby.

"You're still here," she said, and he smiled.

"I still haven't had my coffee and doughnuts."

"Will you leave if I bring them to you?"

"Do you want me to?"

"Well, you *are* taking up space other customers could use."

"There aren't many customers right now."

"There will be." She got up and grabbed his doughnuts and coffee, making sure everything was packaged to go and handing them to him over the counter.

No more men.

She'd promised herself that after she'd walked out on Andrew, but she just couldn't seem to keep herself from looking deep into Ryder's eyes.

"Take the sheriff's advice, Shelby Ann. Be careful," Ryder said, his gaze sweeping over her face like a physical touch. Then he turned and walked out of the bakery, left her there staring after him.

"You going to work or going home? Because right now, you're just in the way," Dottie muttered.

"I'm working. We have two weddings next weekend, remember?" Shelby walked to the kitchen, irritated with Dottie and with her own weakness when it came to Ryder.

What she needed to do, what she had to do, was immerse herself in work, forget everything else for a while.

Fifteen hours later, she was still working as Dottie muttered about die-hard foolishness, locked the front door and left for the night.

Maybe she was right.

Maybe Shelby *would* be better off at home, but working kept her mind off all the things she couldn't change.

Maureen's death.

The cold-eyed man of her nightmares.

She hummed under her breath as she wiped down the display case one last time, rolled the last tray of dough into the walk-in refrigerator to proof over night. She'd make sweet breads from it. Sticky buns and cinnamon rolls and caramel-pecan rolls that she'd bring to church in the morning.

She walked into her tiny office, grabbing her purse from under the desk and catching sight of herself in the small mirror Dottie had hung from the back of the door. A mess. That's what she was. Hair escaping the clips she'd pulled it back with, skin pale and still slightly stained with mascara— she looked gaunt and exhausted and sickly.

And that's exactly how she felt.

A soft sound came from the front of the bakery.

Subtle, but there when there should be nothing.

No sound. No whisper of another's presence.

Shelby's heart thundered in response, her muscles tight with fear as she grabbed a knife from the kitchen and peered into the serving area.

Nothing.

No one.

Just the way it should be.

But the sound came again.

Not inside.

Outside.

And her gaze jumped to the floor-to-ceiling windows, the glass door.

The man standing there.

Medium height.

Medium build.

Something covering his face, distorting his features.

He leaned close to the door handle, seemed intent on something.

Slowly, the door she'd watched Dottie lock opened, the bell above it ringing. Shelby dived for cover, falling onto her hands and knees and crawling toward the back exit, trying desperately to find her cell phone in the overstuffed pocket of her purse.

Please, God, don't let him see me!

But she could hear his feet padding on tile floor, knew that he was coming for her.

Slow and easy, because he knew she had nowhere to run, no one to help.

Please!

But there was no help, nothing but the sound of her heart thundering in her ears and the tap of feet on tile floor.

She lunged for the back door, her shaking fingers barely managing the lock. Cool air slapped her face as she raced out into the dark alley behind the bakery.

Something snagged her shirt.

Someone yanked her back, dragged her deeper into the alley's black shadows.

"Give me your money!" he demanded, pulling the purse from her shoulder.

She didn't waste her breath telling him it was empty of cash. She just shoved into him, using a move she'd learned in the self-defense class Dottie had insisted she take.

He stumbled back, and she lifted the knife, her hand shaking as she did the unthinkable. Plunged it toward her attacker, intent on harming or killing or doing whatever was necessary to make it out alive.

He knocked her hand to the side, the blade barely grazing his arm before it clattered to the ground, curses spewing from his mouth as he dragged something from his pocket.

A gun.

"No more games, lady. We're going back in the bakery, and you're emptying the till for me. Any trouble, and I kill you."

"It's already empty," she said, the sound of traffic on the street beyond the alley a siren's song. All she had to do was run.

A hundred feet, and she'd be out on the street with cars and people and safety.

A hundred feet.

With bullets flying?

Or maybe not.

Maybe he'd go into the bakery by himself. Take what he wanted while she escaped.

Never get in a car with your attacker.

That's what the self-defense teacher had said.

Did the same apply to going in a building with him?

Should she fight to the death? Or go along and pray the guy wouldn't kill her once they got inside?

He grabbed her arm, his fingers cruel and hard as he tugged her back to the door.

She looked into his green eyes, saw intent and something else, something vaguely familiar and completely terrifying.

Coldness.

Emptiness.

The same look she'd seen in the eyes of the guy who'd been jogging near Maureen's place, who had stood in front of the hospital. Only he'd had ice-blue eyes. It couldn't be the same man.

Could it?

Panicked, she slammed her foot into his knee, kicking with enough strength to knock his leg out from under him.

He cursed, swung the gun and aimed it at her face.

No more time to think.

She dived, the explosion of gunfire nearly deafening her.

The bullet whizzed by her, its heat and energy blasting through the small alley.

Run!

She took off, zigzagging like someone in an action thriller. Only this wasn't a movie and it wasn't thrilling.

Terror fueled her, egged her on.

The mouth of the alley just a few feet away, beckoning her.

Another gunshot exploded.

Something slammed into her back, knocked the breath from her lungs. Momentum carried her out into the street. Car horns blared as she stumbled into traffic. Someone shouted. Darkness and light pulsed around her as she fell to the pavement.

Get up!

Keep running!

But life and energy seemed to pour onto the ground, spill into the street.

Blood flowing like a river, and she flowed with it as someone ran toward her, knelt beside her; a stranger with horror in her eyes, talking into a phone, screaming for help as Shelby flowed away.

SIX

"One-twenty-five. One-twenty-six. One-twenty-seven. One-twenty-eigh—" Ryder's phone rang as he neared the end of his workout, and he thought about ignoring it. Just two more push-ups and he'd be done. Finished for the night. But it was late for anyone to be calling. Late for good news anyway. Bad news, that could come at any time.

He grabbed the phone, glanced at the caller ID.

Chance Richardson.

A private investigator with Information Unlimited, Chance had worked with Ryder a few months ago. They hadn't hit it off. After working together to save a woman's life, they'd formed a truce and a friendship of sorts, but they weren't chummy enough for late night phone chats.

"Malone, here. What's up, Richardson?" he asked, grabbing a towel from the weight bench he'd set up in his living room and wiping his brow and chest.

"My mother-in-law just got a call from Dottie Jamieson. They go to church together. She mentioned your name, asked Lila if there was any way to look you up."

"Why?" he asked, worry rearing up and taking hold.

"She wanted you to know that Shelby was taken to the hospital a half hour—"

"What happened?"

"An intruder tried to rob her bakery, and he shot her in the process. She was alert enough when she arrived at the hospital to have staff call Dottie, but Dottie needs transportation to the hospital. She wanted my mother-in-law to take her, but since she mentioned you, and you're closer to the hospital and to Dottie, I thought I'd give you a call first."

"What hospital?" He didn't bother asking who'd shot Shelby, where she'd been shot, what her chances were. Those questions would come after he got to the hospital and made sure she was still alive.

"Deaconess."

"Give me Dottie's address, and tell her I'll pick her up on my way there."

Chance rattled off an address that was halfway between Ryder and the hospital. He didn't want to stop, didn't want to waste a second of time doing anything other than getting to the hospital, but he knew what Shelby would want, and that tied his hands and limited his choices.

"Tell her to be outside the house. If she isn't, I'm going on without her." He hung up before Chance could reply, tugged on a T-shirt and jogged down the four flights of stairs to the apartment complex's parking area.

It took less than two minutes to reach Dottie, but it seemed like an hour.

Seemed as if it took longer than that for her to climb into the Hummer.

She refused his help, of course.

Only her haggard expression and the tears on her cheeks kept Ryder from rushing her.

"You need steps on this thing, boy," she groused as he closed the door, but he could hear the terror behind her words, feel it pulsing through the Hummer as he jumped in, started the engine and sped toward the hospital.

"How bad is she?" he asked as Dottie urged him to drive faster.

"She called me, so she's alive and breathing. They're taking her into surgery. Stopping some internal bleeding. Taking out her spleen. My poor, poor girl." Her voice broke, and Ryder patted her bony knee, regretting it when she winced away.

"She'll be okay."

"I know that," she snapped, but her voice shook.

Ryder pulled into the hospital parking lot, forced himself to wait while Dottie eased out of the Hummer.

"You can move faster than me. You go in there, and you tell those doctors they better save my girl. If they don't…"

He didn't hear the rest of Dottie's threat.

He was across the parking lot and in the emergency room in seconds. A young nurse looked up as he approached the reception desk. "Can I help you, sir?"

"I'm looking for Shelby Simons."

"She's a patient?"

"Yes."

She typed something into the computer, slowly scanning whatever she pulled up, and he wanted to jump over the counter, look for himself.

Finally, she looked up, offered a compassionate smile.

"She's still in surgery."

"Is she—"

"I'm sorry, sir. That's the only information I can give you. Go up to the third-floor surgical unit and wait there. The surgeon will be out to speak with you once Ms. Simons is in recovery."

"Well? Well?" Dottie hobbled in as Ryder jabbed a finger at the elevator button.

"She's still in surgery."

"Still in surgery? What kind of hospital is this?" Dottie shouted, and Ryder was tempted to slam a hand over her mouth.

"The kind that will kick you out if you cause a ruckus."

"I'm not causing anything. I'm asking a reasonable question. Shelby called me twenty minutes ago. Seems to me they should have patched her up by now."

Internal bleeding?

Removing a spleen?

Those things took time, but Ryder didn't say that to Dottie as they made their way to the waiting area. They both knew it, and the weight of their combined worry seemed to fill the small room.

Finally, he couldn't take it anymore.

Not the hushed expectancy of the surgical ward or the loud tapping of Dottie's fingers on the arm-rest of her chair.

"I'm going to find out what's taking so long."

"It's about time," Dottie grumbled as he walked into the hall. He'd track someone down. Find out something.

Wide double doors opened at the end of the hall, and a short round man appeared, his surgical scrubs loosened, a mask hanging from his neck. He met Ryder's eyes, his gaze filled with the same compassion Ryder had seen in the eyes of every doctor and nurse who'd tended him in Afghanistan.

He braced himself for bad news.

Braced himself but didn't want to hear it.

"Are you a relative of Shelby Simons?"

"A friend."

"I won't beat around the bush, then. I'm sure you're anxious to hear how she's doing."

"Yes." And if the doctor didn't start talking

quickly, Ryder might be tempted to shake the information out of him.

"She made it through surgery. The bullet hit her spleen and nicked her liver, but we were able to stop the bleeding. She has a cracked rib, but that should heal well. Barring any unforeseen complications, she should make a full recovery."

"Where is she?" he asked as Dottie hurried into the hallway.

"Room 415. She can only have one visitor at a time, though, and the police are waiting to interview her."

"You go on up, boy. I can wait a few more minutes," Dottie said, something calculating and sly in her eyes.

"What are you up to, Dottie?" Ryder asked, but he was pretty sure he knew. Matchmaking. Just like Shelby had said.

"Just thinking that you'll be a lot better at tracking down the guy who shot my girl than I will be. You'll also be a lot better at meting out justice."

"That's a job for the police." But he wouldn't mind taking it out of their hands. Catching the guy, giving him just a little taste of what it felt like to be on the other side of the gun appealed to Ryder in a way that thrummed through his blood, made him desperate for the hunt.

He jogged up the stairs, trying to work off adrenaline, settle into a better frame of mind before he saw Shelby. His rage would do her no good.

Two police officers stood outside Shelby's door. They eyed him dispassionately as he approached.

"You a friend of the victim?" the shorter officer asked, and Ryder nodded.

"The deputy sheriff is in there. Once he's done—"

Ryder opened the door, walked into the room.

She looked small in the hospital bed, dwarfed by the sheets tugged up around her shoulders. An IV line snaked from her arm, and a heart monitor tracked her racing pulse. Pale. Everything. Cheeks. Lips. The only color in her face the vivid blue of her eyes.

Ryder walked past a tall, hard-faced officer, lifted Shelby's hand. "How are you feeling, Shelby Ann?"

"I'm shot up so full of drugs, I can't feel anything." Her eyes drifted closed, and Ryder met the officer's eyes.

"Ryder Malone." He offered a hand.

"Deputy Sheriff Logan Randal. Spokane County Sheriff's Department. I have a few more questions to ask Ms. Simons. If you'll wait out in the hall—"

"No."

"It wasn't a request, Mr. Malone."

"Nor is it a possibility," he responded, pulling a chair to the bedside and sitting down.

"Don't get yourself thrown in jail on my account, Ryder," Shelby mumbled.

"No one is going to jail, Ms. Simons. Except the person who did this to you, and hopefully, we'll have him in custody soon." Randal gave in without a fight. A guy who picked his battles. Ryder could appreciate that.

"I hope so, because I don't want him showing up at my bakery again." She opened her eyes, wincing as she tried to sit up.

"Hold on. You're going to rip something the doctors just fixed." Ryder pushed the button to adjust the bed, and Shelby winced again.

"You *are* in pain."

"Only when I breathe."

"I'll call the nurse."

"No, you won't. I'm already groggy from whatever they gave me during surgery, and I want to answer Randal's questions. If I don't, how are they going to catch the guy who shot me?"

"Did you get a look at your attacker, Ms. Simons?" Randal cut in smoothly, and Shelby shook her head.

"He had a mask over his face. Some kind of nylon thing that distorted his features. Very creepy." She shuddered, and Ryder lifted her hand, brushing his thumb over her knuckles, trying to warm her chilled skin.

"How about hair color? Eye color?"

"Not his hair, but I saw his eyes. They were green. That surprised me, because…" Her voice trailed off, and she shrugged, wincing at the movement.

"What?" Ryder asked, and she took a deep breath.

"This is going to sound completely paranoid,

but when he walked into the bakery, I was sure he was the guy I saw yesterday morning. But that guy had silvery-blue eyes, so they couldn't be the same, could they?" Shelby's voice drifted off, her eyes closing again, and Ryder met Logan's gaze.

"Contacts?" he asked, and Logan shrugged.

"Or two different people."

"They were the same height and build. They even moved the same, but maybe I just thought that because I was terrified," Shelby said, trying again to sit up, her hospital gown falling off one shoulder, revealing creamy skin and a deep black bruise.

The rage Ryder had been tamping down boiled up and threatened to spill over. He tugged the gown back into place, his heart thundering with anger and something else.

A deep, deep need to protect Shelby.

To keep her from being hurt again.

"Do you have a security camera at your store?" Randal asked, and Shelby shook her head.

"No."

"Too bad. That might have helped. Tell you what. We have a team collecting evidence at the scene. Once we're finished, I'll come back, check in with you again. For now, how about you just rest? The sheriff already put in a call to the state police. A composite-sketch artist will meet with you as soon as you're up to it. Once we have the sketch, we can release it to the public. Hopefully, that will make it easier to find our perp."

"Okay." Shelby's eyes were already closed again, her breathing deep and even.

"Can I speak to you out in the hall for a minute, Ryder?" Randal asked.

"Sure."

Shelby grabbed his hand, her heartbeat jumping, the monitor beeping loudly. "Are you coming back?"

And he knew he had to.

Come back.

Again and again and again to Shelby's side.

Because there was something about her that called to him, and he couldn't deny it. Couldn't refuse it.

"Count on it," he responded as he eased his hand from hers and followed Randal into the hall.

SEVEN

She just needed to suck it in a little more.

Just a little.

Shelby exhaled every bit of breath from her lungs, squeezed in her stomach and *just* managed to close the button of her shirtwaist dress.

Stupid bandages.

She frowned at her reflection, unhappy with the tightness of the dress, but unwilling to wear one of her brighter-colored, looser-fitting outfits to Maureen's funeral. A funeral she was going to no matter what anyone said.

It had been one day since Shelby had left the hospital.

Four days since she'd been shot.

Time to step back into the world, regain control of her bakery and her life. Despite Dottie's protests, despite her mother's insistence that Shelby fly to California to recuperate for a month, Shelby was going to attend the funeral, and then she was going back to work.

But first she had to make it out the front door.

She slid her feet into two-inch heels, wobbled to the door, and grabbed the collar and leash from the coat hook. A neighbor had fed and walked Mazy while Shelby was in the hospital, but the poor little dog hadn't been happy about it. She'd chewed up both of Shelby's throw pillows and eaten half a roll of paper towels.

"Come on, Mazy. Today is the day. I know it's hard, but you're going to have to say goodbye to Maureen." She crouched to snap the collar around the dog's neck.

Now all she had to do was stand up and walk out the door into the bright spring day.

Too bad moving made her break out in a cold sweat.

Too bad her back burned and her rib ached.

Too bad she couldn't have downed a couple of the painkillers the doctor had prescribed, but taking them would have meant not driving, and she was going to drive, because she was *not* going to ask anyone for a ride.

Especially not anyone named Ryder.

Ryder, who'd arrived at the hospital every night at six. Who'd snuck her pizza when she'd moaned about being hungry for real food. Who'd sat by her side during the worst moments of pain.

Ryder, who made her insides shake and her brain turn to mush and who made her forget that she'd sworn off men.

No. She wouldn't call to ask for a ride even though Ryder had told her she could call for anything.

She was going to do this herself. Man up and face the fear. That's what Grandmother Beulah would have expected from the granddaughter she'd willed the Cadillac to.

Of course, Grandmother Beulah had never been shot in the back.

Shelby took a deep breath, opened the door.

Bright sunlight splashed across the lawn the neighbor's son had mowed for her the previous day. Tulips peeked up from the dark soil of the flower-beds she'd planted last spring. Everything was as it should be on her quiet street. No stealthy movement or unusual noise. Nothing alarming. The police had assured her that she was safe. That the man with the green eyes couldn't possibly be the guy she'd seen running from Maureen's street. He'd demanded cash, after all. Made it clear he was there to rob Shelby.

A robbery gone wrong.

Nothing at all to do with Maureen's murder.

But Shelby didn't feel safe.

She hadn't felt safe in days.

She hurried to Old Blue, her body screaming in pain as she jumped into the car, slammed the door and locked it. Mazy whined and panted in the passenger seat as she drove the ten miles to the funeral home.

Empty parking lot.

Nothing to indicate a funeral was about to take place.

Had Shelby come on the wrong date?

The way her week had been going, that wouldn't be surprising. She got out of the car anyway, leading Mazy across the parking lot and into the silent building.

An usher stood at a podium beside the door, and he smiled as Shelby approached.

"You're here for the Lewis funeral?"

"Yes."

"First door on the left, but I'm afraid you'll have to leave the dog in your car."

"She's Maureen's dog."

"You'll still have to leave her in the car."

"But—"

"Ma'am, I'm sorry, but that's our rule. Some people are allergic to dogs, and we don't want to make this time any more stressful than it needs to be."

He had a point, and Shelby would have given in quickly if she weren't so terrified of going back outside.

"Maureen would have wanted her here."

"The deceased left no indication of that, so I'm afraid we'll have to follow policy." His smile had tightened, but he managed to keep it intact. Good for him.

Shelby's smile had failed four days ago.

It didn't seem ready to return.

Fear hummed along her nerves as she walked Mazy back to the car, her eyes scanning the street, the trees that sheltered the lush lawn, the people who strolled along the sidewalk. *He* could be there. He *might* be there. She'd never know it, either. Not until the bullet slammed into her body, carried her along its trajectory.

Killed her.

It would be quite an irony to die in the parking lot of a funeral home.

That kind of dramatic, over-the-top end was exactly what Grandmother Beulah would have preferred to having a heart attack in her sleep.

Shelby, on the other hand, was hoping for exactly the type of end her grandmother had gotten. Peaceful. Quiet. Slipping easily into the next part of her journey at the ripe old age of ninety-seven.

"Get in, Mazy." She patted the seat of the Caddy, but Mazy dug in her paws and refused to budge.

"Mazy, really. I'm not supposed to lift you, so hop in." She leaned down and nudged the dog. Pain edged in over the fear, churning in her stomach. She felt sick and dizzy, her skin clammy, her heart chugging too fast and hard.

So, maybe she wouldn't die in the parking lot.

Maybe she'd just pass out.

"Please, Mazy. Cooperate." She slid her hands

under the dog's belly, lifted her, felt the burn of stitched skin stretching as she tried to get to her feet.

"You're not supposed to be lifting anything." Ryder's voice spilled into the quiet afternoon, and she looked up, nearly fell over as she tried to see his face.

"Where did you come from?"

"My apartment." He grabbed her arm, tugged her to her feet, somehow pulling Mazy from her hands and setting her on the Caddy's seat at the same time.

"That's not what I mean, and you know it," she grumbled, closing the door on Mazy's excited yaps.

"Grumpy, Shelby Ann?" He watched her through deep brown eyes, his dark suit perfectly tailored to his muscular frame, and Shelby's whole being sighed with longing. She wanted to step into his arms, tell him how scared she was, how glad that he'd shown up.

"I'm tired, and I'm in pain, and I don't feel like dealing with Mazy." She turned from his dark gaze, wobbled across the parking lot. She should have worn sneakers. They'd have made for a more dignified retreat.

"You're tired and in pain, because you're supposed to be home in bed recovering. What you're not supposed to be doing is driving. Fortunately, my apartment is close enough to walk here, so I can drive us both to the cemetery in your car." Ryder opened the door, the spicy, masculine scent of his cologne drifting around Shelby. She resisted the urge to inhale deeply, pull in his scent and make a memory of it.

"You've been talking to Dottie."

"She called because she was sure you'd show up here. I was sure you'd use a little common sense and stay home."

"How could I? Today is Maureen's funeral. We were friends."

"She has other friends." Ryder offered a curt nod in the direction of the usher, nudged Shelby into the viewing room.

"I know," Shelby whispered, because she felt compelled to keep her voice down as people trickled in, walked by the closed casket and stared at the flower arrangements.

"Anyone here you know?" Ryder asked, and Shelby shook her head.

"Maureen and I didn't run in the same social circles."

"How'd you meet, then?" He walked her to a row of chairs and urged her to sit.

"She came into the bakery the day I opened and bought every one of my cheese Danishes. They were her favorite. She came in every week after that. Five years, and she never missed a Monday Danish run." Shelby blinked back tears as she stood and walked to the mahogany coffin. Flowers cascaded over the dark wood. Beautiful lily of the valley and gorgeous white roses.

Shelby touched a velvety bloom, her fingers caressing the silken petal. "I'm so sorry that I couldn't save you, Maureen," she whispered, and Ryder slid his arm around her waist, his touch light and gentle.

"Come on. Let's sit back down before you fall down."

"I'm not going to fall." But her legs were shaky, and she let Ryder lead her back to the chair, leaned her head down on her knees, the stitches in her back pulling, her muscles protesting.

"You really should have followed doctor's orders and stayed home, Shelby Ann." He pressed a cool palm to the back of her neck, his rough, callused skin comforting.

The touch of a very good and very old friend.

But he wasn't even really a friend at all. He was...

Ryder, and she couldn't put a label to him.

Wasn't sure she dared try.

"You're looking at me like I've grown two heads," he said, and she realized she was staring straight into his dark eyes.

"Just wondering why you're here."

"Why wouldn't I be?"

"You didn't know Maureen."

"I know you," he said, taking the seat beside her, his long legs stretched out, his thigh muscles pressing against his dark slacks.

"Ryder—" She wanted to tell him that he needed to stop whatever he was doing. Stop the caring and the concern and the sweet words. Stop convincing her heart of something that could never be true, but the service began, music swelling from a piano near the back of the room, a few of Maureen's friends speaking fondly of her, a pastor speaking of eternity. Fifty years of life summed up in twenty minutes. The music swelled again, people spilling out to head for the cemetery. Tears dripped down Shelby's cheeks, and suddenly, she was leaning into Ryder's chest, his suit jacket muffling the sound of her quiet sobs.

Had she gone to him?

Had he come to her?

It didn't matter, because she was there, in his arms, his hand making small circles on her shoulder, his quiet murmurs filling her ear. "She would want you to celebrate what she was, Shelby. Not mourn for what she can't be."

"I know."

"Then stop crying." He brushed tears from her cheeks, his palm rough and warm against her cool skin, his dark eyes filled with sadness.

"Have you ever lost someone you cared about, Ryder?" she asked, because she wanted to know what made his eyes so dark and bleak.

"Four of my military buddies. We were SEALs together. Ten of us. Six of us survived the explosion that took their lives. I was one of the lucky ones. Come on. We need to get to the cemetery."

"Ryder, wait." She grabbed his arm, felt tension in his muscles, but his voice was gentle, his gaze soft as he answered.

"It was six years ago, Shelby Ann. I'm over the worst of it, but I do know what it feels like to lose someone you respect, admire and care deeply about. Come on." He tugged her to Old Blue and helped her into the passenger seat. She didn't bother arguing about who was going to drive. She was too tired, too sad. Because of Maureen. Because of Ryder's comrades. Because she wanted to reach out and touch Ryder's hand, tell him how sorry she was, but her throat was too clogged with tears, and she wasn't nearly brave enough to risk everything that reaching out might mean.

Hadn't she learned anything from her thrice-married-and-divorced mother? From her globe-trotting, heartbreaker sister? From her tough-as-nails grandmother? From scarred and tattered Dottie?

From her own experiences with the men that she'd wanted desperately to believe in and who had proven just how foolish believing in anyone was?

Of course she had.

Rely on yourself, because men will only disappoint you.

That was the Simons family's motto, but she'd never really believed it. Not even when her college sweetheart had broken up with her because he wanted to date her roommate. Finally, though, she *did* believe it.

Andrew had convinced her.

She'd tried.

She'd failed.

She wouldn't try again.

Coward, her heart seemed to whisper as Ryder turned the key in the ignition and Old Blue roared to life. *Coward,* it whispered again as he met her gaze, smiled into her eyes. She ignored him, because she *was* a coward, and every minute she spent near Ryder just proved it more. She turned to stare out the window as he followed the funeral processional to the grave site.

EIGHT

Ryder surveyed the cemetery as the pastor bestowed a few last words on Maureen. He saw no sign that unexpected guests were watching the proceedings, but that didn't mean none were.

Maureen's name was synonymous with titillating true-crime tales, and there was no doubt some of the hundreds of mourners were fans anxious to see how the bestselling author's final chapter would play out rather than mourners sad to say goodbye. Fans weren't who Ryder was worried about, though.

Maureen's murderer was.

The person who'd bludgeoned her to death. Aside from the skull fracture, the medical examiner had found multiple broken bones. Forearm, ribs, cheek, jaw and nose. Ryder hadn't had the heart to tell Shelby that. Not when she was still recovering, but eventually someone would. If not Ryder, the sheriff or deputy sheriff. Both men hovered at the edge of the grave site, shifting restlessly as they eyed the mourners. Like Ryder, they expected the killer to show, and they were desperate to catch him.

More than likely, he was in the crowd, relishing the tears that were being shed. Ryder's chest tightened at the thought, anger gnawing at him. The perp needed to be caught before he hurt someone else.

Before he hurt Shelby.

Again.

Blue eyes, green eyes, brown eyes. None of it mattered, because Ryder was absolutely sure the man Shelby had seen the morning of Maureen's death was the man who'd staged a robbery at Just Desserts and shot her in the back.

He followed her as she placed a white rose on Maureen's coffin.

"Goodbye for now, my friend," she said quietly and moved to the edge of the canopied area. Sunlight poured over her, bathing her dark hair in red and gold and highlighting the deep hollows beneath her cheekbones. Dressed in a simple dress that hugged her curves, she looked beautiful and heartbroken. She hadn't been sleeping well, hadn't been eating well. She didn't need to say it for Ryder to know the truth.

"You okay?" he asked, sliding both arms around her waist and tugging her a step closer. Her eyes widened, but she didn't protest or try to move away.

"I will be. I saw the sheriff and deputy sheriff. Are they hoping Maureen's murderer will show up?"

"Yes."

"Do you think he will?"

"I *hope* he will."

"He's not here now. At least, the guy I saw jogging that morning isn't here." She stepped away, breaking the contact between them.

"You're sure?"

"Positive. I've been looking, too." She shivered, rubbing her arms against a chill Ryder couldn't feel.

"Here." He started to pull off his jacket, but Shelby grabbed his arm.

"Don't. The last thing this crowd needs is to see a bulked-up Hercules wearing a gun and holster."

"'Bulked-up Hercules'? I'm not sure if I should be flattered or insulted by that, Shelby Ann."

"Neither." She blushed, the pink tinge in her cheeks only adding to her beauty.

"Then what should I be?"

"Impressed that I came up with such a clever description? Look, there's Maureen's son." She quickly changed the subject, gesturing to the casket and a tall, dark-haired man that stood before it, his head bowed, his eyes hidden by dark glasses. Early to midthirties. Close to six feet. Maybe a hundred and eighty pounds. He looked too old to be a fifty-year-old woman's son.

"She must have had him young."

"She was seventeen. His father was her first and only marriage. She had Hunter six months later. A big mistake, she said."

"The marriage or her son?"

"The marriage mostly. Although things were

strained between Maureen and Hunter. She wasn't a very maternal person, and I think she caused some damage to their relationship when he was younger. She never told me the details, though."

"Maybe we should ask Hunter." He took a step toward the man, but Shelby grabbed his arm.

"You can't ask a man why he didn't get along with his mother while he's at her funeral," she hissed, and Ryder almost told her she was wrong. He could ask anyone anything if it meant keeping Shelby safe.

Maureen had been killed.

Someone knew why.

Someone knew who.

Maybe Maureen's son was the key.

"Come on. I need to get home and get changed. I want to go to the bakery to check—"

"You're not going to the bakery, Shelby," he said.

"Of course I am."

"Dottie and the rest of your staff have everything under control, and you'll only be in the way."

"Is that what Dottie told you to say?"

"Only if you insisted on going back to work before you were ready."

"I *am* ready. Maybe not physically," she admitted reluctantly. "But mentally."

"You need to be both."

"You don't understand, Ryder." She started walking back to Old Blue, her movements stiff with pain.

"Then explain it to me."

"I'm afraid. When I'm awake, I think I see the

guy who shot me around every corner and lurking in every shadow. When I'm asleep, he's there, too. Always at the bakery, rushing at me with a gun. Every day I don't go back and prove to myself that he's gone, the fear builds. Eventually, it will be so big that I won't be able to go back, no matter how much I want to."

"Okay."

"Okay what?" She leaned against Blue's door, her eyes shadowed and wary.

"I'll take you to the bakery. Dottie will probably cut off my doughnut supply for life, but I'll take you."

"Thanks, but I don't need you to take me. I can manage on my own. It's what I've been doing for years." She offered her first real smile of the day, her eyes crinkling at the corners, a dimple flashing in her left cheek. He ran a finger over it, watching as her pupils dilated.

"You're beautiful when you smile."

"You've been using that word a lot today," she responded, getting in Blue's passenger seat, wincing as she settled in.

"*Beautiful?* What's wrong with that?"

"I'm not beautiful, Ryder. Cute, maybe. Pretty, sometimes. Beautiful, never."

"Who told you that?" he asked as he got into driver's seat and started Blue's engine.

"I lived with three beautiful people growing up. My grandmother was an actress. My mother was

Miss California. My sister is a runway model. I know beautiful, and I'm not. It doesn't bother me, so you don't have to try to convince me that I am what I'm not."

"Okay."

"You're the king of the one-word responses today, you know that?"

"And you're still grumpy."

"True." She sighed, leaning her head back against the leather seat. "I am also letting you drive again, and I'm not sure why."

"Because Old Blue runs better for me?"

"She does *not* run better for you. The weather is warming up. She always starts better in warm weather. The thing is…" Her eyes widened. "That's him!" she shouted, grabbing Ryder's arm and leaning so far toward him, she was nearly in his lap. Silky hair brushed his chin, her hand clutched his thigh, and he was pretty sure lava flowed in his belly.

"Who?"

"The guy I saw the morning Maureen died. He's right there! Near that statue!" She jabbed her finger past his nose.

Several large statues decorated grave sites. Ryder scanned marble angels and stone figures, his attention caught by movement near the edge of the cemetery. Nothing concrete. Just the feeling that something had scurried out of sight. Could have been a bird or a squirrel, but the hair on the back of his neck stood on end, his pulse jumping with adrenaline. Thick trees offered plenty of cover for anyone who might have been there, their spring-rich branches shielding the area beyond.

"Stay in the car. I'm going to get the sheriff and Randal and take a look."

"You can't—"

"Stay!"

"I'm not a dog, Ryder, and I don—"

He shut the door, left her talking to Mazy.

He ran toward the statue, gesturing for the sheriff and deputy sheriff to follow. They sprinted toward him, catching up as he reached the edge of the cemetery.

"Did you see something?" Logan asked.

"Shelby saw our perp. He was behind this statue." Ryder ducked behind the stone angel, searching the ground for signs that someone had been there.

The sheriff crouched beside him, pointed at compressed grass and a lone broken dandelion. "Looks like someone was here, but it could have been anyone."

"Shelby is convinced it was him." Ryder scanned the copse of trees, moving around thick trunks and out into an open field, Logan right behind him. Thick woods were to the left, vivid green grass to the right and ahead, sloping down to a narrow road that wove its way through the cemetery grounds. Several cars sat near the edge of the road and a few mourners dotted the area. None caught his attention. No one moved quickly. Nothing indicated that someone had run down the slope and jumped in a car.

"The sheriff is heading back to check on Shelby. How about we split up, Malone? You want to check out the cemetery or the woods?"

"I'll try the woods." It seemed like the most likely path for a perp who wanted to disappear quickly, and Ryder wanted first shot at the guy. He'd work by the book, but that didn't mean he couldn't ask a few questions and demand a few answers.

The woods were as thick as he'd imagined, tree trunk pressed close to tree trunk, the heavy scent of pine and decaying leaves filling his nose as he moved. Adrenaline pumped through him, his heart beating quickly in response.

Something moved in the shadows to his left, and he froze, his hand dropping to the gun concealed beneath his suit jacket. Another movement. Subtle. Stealthy. Coming toward him rather than moving away.

Ryder stepped behind a thick pine. Waiting.

A branch broke.

Fabric brushed against tree branches.

Close.

He tensed, holding back, practicing the patience he'd learned as a SEAL. Breath stilling, pulse slowing, everything in him ready and waiting.

Shuffled footfall. Leaves displaced. A hint of movement that let him know the time was right.

He lunged, his thigh screaming as he threw himself at the dark shadow, his arms tightening around wiggling, struggling humanity.

Hints of summer and sunshine floated on the air. Vanilla and chocolate and...

Shelby.

"I told you to stay in the car," he nearly shouted, all his hard-won, hard-earned patience failing as he looked into her terrified eyes, imagined her lying in the trees, her body limp and lifeless.

"I was worried about you."

"Worried about *me?* I was a SEAL for ten years! I faced enemy fire more times than I can count. You should have been worried about yourself. What if I'd pulled my weapon? What if I'd shot you?" He eased his hold, smoothing his fingers over the red marks he'd left on her wrist.

"You're too careful to let something like that happen."

True, but that wasn't the point.

"What if someone else had been waiting in these trees? What if you'd run into the perp out here?"

"I didn't."

"But you could have."

"I know," she finally conceded. "I guess I just wasn't thinking straight. I kept seeing Maureen's house in flames and imagining you lying dead in the woods. I didn't think I could live with the guilt if something happened to you."

"Everything okay over here?" The sheriff tromped

through the woods, and Shelby looked relieved to see him coming.

"We're fine."

"Glad to hear it. I was worried when I got to your car and didn't see you there. A woman in your position shouldn't be wandering around alone."

"A woman in my position?"

"You may have seen a murderer, Ms. Simons. And if so, he saw you. Seeing as how that's the case, you can't be too careful. Of course, you're fortunate in your choice of friends. I'm sure Malone can hook you up with a security system at your house and your business."

"Good idea, Sheriff. Why don't we go get started on that now, Shelby?"

"I don't need—"

"You'd be foolish not to take him up on his offer, young lady. Personal Securities Incorporated is one of the best security contractors in the country. Did you know that?"

"No." Shelby met Ryder's eyes, and he shrugged. It was true. His company *was* among the top five in the nation, but he didn't expect that to impress Shelby. She'd never needed high-level security, probably hadn't ever even thought about it.

"Well, it is. So, like I said, take him up on his offer. We're running patrols by your place, but a good security system will help our efforts. By the way, that sketch artist I told you about will be in this Friday. I'll send a patrol car to get you at ten in the morning. Does that work for you?" The sheriff continued talking while he led them back to grave site.

"That's fine." Shelby's response was sober, and Ryder wondered if she'd finally realized just how much of her freedom she was going to have to give up in order to stay safe.

"Great. I'm anxious to get the composite. If we're lucky, we may be able to match it with someone already in the system."

"I don't believe in luck, Sheriff," she responded, dropping into Blue's passenger seat, her face colorless.

"Well, whatever you believe in, you'd better pray it's good to you, because the guy who murdered Maureen knew what he was doing. He killed her and destroyed every bit of forensic evidence he might have left. You're the last loose end. I doubt he's going to let you keep hanging."

"I'll have a security system put in, Sheriff, and I'll be careful. Now, if you don't mind, I'm exhausted, and I really need to leave."

"Of course." The sheriff closed Blue's door and speared Ryder with a hard look.

"When is the security system going in?"

"Today."

"Good, because I've got a bad feeling about things."

"You and me both," Ryder responded, watching

as Sheriff Jones made his way back to Maureen's grave site.

Empty-handed, but Ryder didn't think it was because the perp hadn't been hanging around. He had been, watching from his hiding place behind the statue.

Had he purposely showed himself to Shelby, or had he made a mistake?

Ryder hoped it was the latter. One mistake meant there would be others, and mistakes would make it easier to track the guy down.

He got into Blue, driving away from the cemetery, outlining the rest of the day in his mind.

Shelby's home security system first. Then the one at the bakery. Maybe neither would be needed, but caution kept people alive.

In Ryder's business, it was better to overreact than to underreact. Better to plan for a war rather than a skirmish.

Because anything could be around the next corner.

A friend.

An enemy.

A booby trap.

He'd learned that the hard way, and his thigh screamed a reminder as he stepped on the gas and merged onto the highway.

NINE

Double-paned windows.

Floodlights over the front and back yards.

Motion-detecting security system tied directly to Ryder's company headquarters.

New locks on all the doors.

Shelby was willing to do all those things, but there was no way in the world—*ever*—that she was going to be escorted from place to place by Ryder. Her poor heart couldn't take it.

She had to put the brakes on, come to a dead halt before she fell over the precipice.

Her hand shook as she set a kettle on her 1940s stove. A hot cup of tea, a couple of painkillers and a few hours at the bakery, that's what she needed.

It was *all* she needed.

She was going to march outside and tell Ryder that just as soon as she finished her tea. He'd gone out there after he'd finished talking to the eight-member team he'd called in to replace her windows, set up her security system and put new locks on the doors.

One day's work.

That's what Ryder had said after he'd walked her through the house, shown her every vulnerability, every weakened defense.

Next thing she knew, she'd been converged on by a vanload of buff men and women all eager to do exactly what Ryder told them.

She poured hot water into her teacup and dunked in a bag of ginger tea. She sipped the tea, her back aching with a ferocity that left her breathless.

She wanted to crawl into bed, pull the covers over her head and try to forget the past week, but she hadn't been kidding when she'd told Ryder she had to go to the bakery. Fear was an insidious beast, and it would consume her if she let it.

Stick your head in the sand and someone might just come along and step on it.

That's what Grandmother Beulah had always said, and Shelby had every intention of keeping that from happening.

She placed the tea on the counter and walked up to her room, trying to ignore the sound of hammers and power tools and voices. She was going to change into something that didn't cut off her breathing or dig into her stitches, and then she was going to demand that Ryder take her to the bakery.

It took a little longer than usual to change. Everything hurt. Her ribs. Her back. Her head.

Moving.

She pulled on soft, faded jeans that seemed just a

little looser than they'd been the last time she'd worn them, and gently maneuvered a white T-shirt over her head. She had a clean apron at work, so she left the one she'd hung from the bedpost there.

She didn't bother with refreshing her makeup. She'd be in the kitchen anyway, tucked away from the world and all its complications. Just Shelby and the stuff she really understood, like yeast and dough and flour and sugar. Those things were so much less complicated than people.

She pulled her hair back in a headband, eyeing her pale skin and the circles beneath her eyes. A week of guilt and fear had taken its toll, but she was ready to put it all behind her.

Maureen was gone.

No way to go back and undo that.

Shelby had to move on.

Just like she'd done so many times before.

She'd perfected the technique.

Get up. Get going. Keep going.

Until one day, the thing that hurt so much didn't hurt quite as much anymore.

She blinked back hot tears, the sound of some sort of power tool ringing in her ears and vibrating through the floorboards.

Time to go.

Let Ryder's team do whatever security thing he'd demanded. She'd come home to a different house and, hopefully, bring a better mood.

"I'm leaving, girl. You be good," Shelby called to

Mazy, who cowered beneath the bed, the noise and people too much for her.

Shelby wouldn't have minded cowering with her, but Simons women were tough. They faced their troubles head-on. They did not turn tail and run at the first hint of danger.

Not that any of them had ever been in danger of more than a hangnail.

She grabbed her purse from the kitchen table and walked to the back door, staring out into the bright afternoon. She needed to find Ryder and tell him she was ready to go, but he'd told her he'd be working outside, and she was afraid to leave the safety of the house.

She took a deep breath, stepped out onto the oversize deck. The yard looked as it always did, steeply sloped and dotted with tall trees. When she'd purchased the house, she'd imagined children sledding down the hill in the winter, rolling down it in the spring. Imagined spending hours on the deck, cooking and laughing and making memories.

Now all she could picture was *him*.

Standing behind the trees.

Waiting with gun drawn and aimed at her heart.

"Going somewhere?" The question came out of nowhere, and she screamed, turning so quickly, she nearly toppled down the deck stairs. She grabbed the railing to steady herself, and looked up into Ryder's deep brown eyes.

"I was looking for you."

"Here I am. What do you need?" He took her hand, gently pulled her back into the kitchen.

You.

The answer danced on the tip of her tongue, but she swallowed it down.

She did *not* need him.

She needed to go to the bakery to prove that she could, and then she needed to bake.

"I need to get back to work."

"I was hoping you'd change your mind about that."

"I didn't."

"Then I'll take you. I need to check on the team that's working there anyway."

"You already have a team at the bakery?"

"Yes."

"Dottie's probably having a fit."

"I told them to lock her in the walk-in if she gave them any trouble."

"You didn't!"

"You're right, but I thought about it." He led her through the house and outside. The new windows were already in, the lights were up. Aside from a guy sitting on the porch, staring at a computer screen and frowning, the house looked normal.

"We online yet?" Ryder asked as they walked past, and the dark-haired young man shook his head.

"Five more minutes."

"Good. Lock up and bring the keys to the other location when the team is finished here."

"Will do." He bent back over the screen, and Ryder hurried Shelby into Old Blue.

"What's he working on?" she asked as Ryder opened the door.

"Do you need your apron?" he responded, closing the door before she could respond.

"What's he working on, Ryder?" she asked again as soon as he got into the car.

"Nothing you need to worry about."

"If you're saying that, then of course I need to worry about it."

"He was tapping into an information database."

"What information and what database?"

"Sometimes a little knowledge is plenty, Shelby Ann," he muttered, pulling out of the driveway.

"It's my life, and I want to have some control over it."

"You have all the control."

"Then why is a team of people setting up a security system at Just Desserts before I've approved it? And why are *you* driving Old Blue while I sit in the driver's seat? And why aren't you telling me what that guy was doing?" Her voice broke on the last word, but she refused to cry. That, at least, she could control.

She hoped.

To her surprise, Ryder didn't respond, just kept driving, his hands loose on Blue's steering wheel, his gaze focused straight ahead.

When he pulled into the parking lot of Just Des-

serts, Shelby grabbed the door handle, ready to run
for the kitchen and her baking supplies, but she
couldn't move fast, and she'd barely pushed the door
open when Ryder grabbed her shoulder, pulling her
back into the car.

"Don't go away mad, Shelby Ann."

"I'm not mad."

"Liar." He smiled gently, tracing her frown with
a rough, warm finger.

What was it with the man and touching?

Didn't he know that every touch seared into her
soul, made rational thought nearly impossible?
Didn't he understand just how tempted she was to
let herself slide full tilt over the edge and into free
fall?

Didn't he understand just how terrifying that
made him?

"What do you want from me, Ryder?" she asked,
and his smile fell away.

"For now? Just to keep you safe."

"And later?"

"I guess we'll both have to decide that. Come on.
You need to get back into the bakery, and I need to
check on my crew's progress."

"You still haven't told me what that guy was
doing."

"I know. Do you think Dottie will hand over a
couple of doughnuts without complaining when I
get in there?" He walked around the side of the car,
his hands gentle as he slid them around her waist

and helped her out, supporting her weight when she swayed.

"Your plan isn't going to work, Ryder."

"Plan?" He raised a sandy eyebrow, his eyes glittering in the late-afternoon sunlight.

"To keep me off balance and distracted."

"If I were trying to distract you, we wouldn't be standing around talking about it." His gaze dropped to her lips and heat zipped through her belly, landed right square in her heart.

It pounded and flipped and danced, carrying her closer to the precipice she wanted to avoid.

"I'm not easily distracted, Ryder."

"No?" He leaned down, his lips so close to hers, she could feel the warmth of his breath. She wanted to close her eyes, sway toward him, let whatever would happen happen, but she wasn't that big of a fool.

"No. Come on. Let's get those doughnuts."

"You're running away," he called out as she tried to hurry to the bakery door, and she didn't argue, because it was true.

She was running as fast as her beat-up, stitched-up, aching body would move.

Ryder still made it to the door before she did, holding it open as she stepped into the bakery. The store overflowed with people who greeted her as she walked inside. She knew most of them by name, but she didn't pause to chat, didn't look over her shoulder to see if Ryder followed.

She knew he was there.

Knew it by the warmth that spread along her nape, the heat that seeped through her. She sidled past Dottie, ignoring her hard look, offered Zane a quick smile and grabbed a spare apron from a hook on the wall.

Vanilla.

Chocolate.

Cinnamon.

Sugar.

The scents were familiar and comforting, washing over her as she gingerly tugged the apron over her head.

This she knew.

This she understood.

This world of pans and baking products and business.

This she could handle.

She'd let Ryder do his thing. She'd do hers. Eventually, the guy who'd shot her and killed Maureen would be found and put in jail. Life would go on. Ryder would move on.

And Shelby would move right back into her routine. Only, she'd have a new security system in her house and her bakery, and a new hole in her heart.

She frowned, working flour, water, butter and sugar into a sweet dough, her muscles tightening and protesting with every movement.

She didn't care, didn't stop, because losing herself in bread dough was a whole lot less painful than losing herself in Ryder.

She had to keep that in mind.

She *would* keep it in mind.

Two strikes and she was out.

There wouldn't be a third, but every time Shelby looked into Ryder's eyes, she couldn't help wishing there could be.

TEN

Maybe work hadn't been such a good idea.

Shelby winced as she lifted the oversize round base of Terri Anderson's wedding cake.

"It's already seven o'clock, Shelby Ann. You said you were leaving at four. Go home and let me handle that cake. I'll take the bus home when I'm done," Dottie groused, but they both knew she couldn't have lifted the cake. At seventy-eight, Dottie was just beginning to slow down. What she lacked in energy, she made up for in attitude, and she'd been shoving it down Shelby's throat since the bakery closed two hours ago.

"You've been here since three this morning. You're the one who should go home, and you know that Zane said he'd come back and pick you up when you were ready. You don't have to take the bus." Shelby panted as she hefted the second layer of the cake and slid it into the walk-in fridge with the other, a sharp pain shooting through her back at the movement.

She groaned, rubbing the muscles beneath her stitches but finding no relief.

"See? You've reinjured yourself."

"I'll be fine. I just need a minute." She wiped cold sweat from her brow.

"You wouldn't need a minute if you were home in bed where you should be."

"Point taken, Dottie. Now, call Zane, grab your stuff and go home. I'll work better without you standing over me." Shelby sighed as she lifted the final tier of the cake. The crumb coat would harden overnight, and she'd cover the cake in rich buttercream the next day.

No fondant for Terri.

Just a few dozen sugar flowers that Shelby had to craft before the nuptials the following day. She'd promised Terri she'd get it done when the bride had called frantic after hearing the news about Shelby's hospitalization.

Seventeen hours before she had to deliver the cake, and the flowers weren't made, the cakes had *just* been crumb coated, and she wasn't sure she'd be able to lift the tiers when it came time to stack them, but Shelby would finish.

It was going to be a long night.

She glanced at her clipboard, flipped through to the other cake orders. Just the one for the coming weekend.

Then three more for the following weekend.

By that time, she should be feeling more herself and less like a slug.

She grabbed the tools she needed, set them on the counter and pulled a chair from her office, ignoring Dottie's glowering stare. Usually, she didn't sit while she worked, but desperate times called for desperate measures.

"You're not going to make those flowers tonight. You're going to drive me home." It wasn't a question, and Shelby chose to ignore Dottie's grumbled comment.

"Are you ignoring me, Shelby Ann? Because if you are, your poor grandmother will turn over in her grave. The disgrace of knowing that her granddaughter wasn't raised well enough—"

"Dottie, please, go call Zane."

"I don't want that tattooed kid to drive me. I want you to."

"You sound like a spoiled child, you know that?"

"I'm way too old to be called a child."

"Not if you're acting like one."

"I'm an old lady, Shelby Ann, and I want family to bring me home. Is that too much to ask?" Dottie changed tactics, and Shelby smiled at her predictability.

"You want to ride with me, then you're going to have to wait, because I can't go home until these flowers are done."

"Do them in the morning."

"The wedding is tomorrow night, which means I'm already a day behind where I should be. The flowers need to be made and then painted tonight, because they need to dry for at least—"

"I know how long they need to dry, girl. And I know that morning is plenty early enough to paint them."

"I don't like to do them the same day as the wedding, Dottie. You know that."

"I also know that you're not up to sitting here for the next five hours making flowers. You call Terri and tell her that the cake is going to have piping and icing roses. That'll be good enough."

"It's her wedding, and she's my friend. I'm not going to give her something less than what she asked for." Besides, the truth was she really didn't want to go home. Not when she wasn't sure who would be there or what she'd find.

Bars on the windows, maybe?

Ryder making himself comfortable on her sofa?

Ryder.

At least he hadn't hung around the bakery. He'd walked her in, done his security thing with his crew, said something about a meeting with the sheriff and left.

He hadn't returned. Which should have been fine with Shelby, but somehow it wasn't.

She frowned as she rolled gum paste and started the first set of petals.

Five hours.

That's about how long it would take to make and paint the flowers.

By the time she finished, the sun would be down, darkness cloaking the street and the sidewalk and anyone who might be lying in wait. She shuddered, fear clawing at her gut, Dottie's soft snores drifting through the room.

Dottie's snores?

She glanced at her grandmother's best and oldest friend.

Head back against the wall, her bluish curls somehow deflated, her skin papery and pale, her bones brittle.

It wouldn't take much to break one.

Wouldn't take much to put a bullet through one, either.

What Shelby could easily recover from might kill a woman of Dottie's age.

Not a good thought.

Not good at all.

"Dottie! Wake up!"

"Huh? What?"

"You fell asleep." *Now you're going to get up and go home, so whoever tried to kill me won't kill you.*

"I was just resting my eyes, Shelby Ann. Now, why'd you have to go and ruin that?"

"Because, it's nearly eight, and I want to bring you home before the sun goes down."

"You said you weren't leaving until you were done."

"I changed my mind. Come on. Let's get out of here." Shelby winced as she stood to grab her purse, blood pulsing in the bruised flesh that surrounded the gunshot wound, reminding her of just how quickly the peaceful bakery could turn into a nightmare.

"You're taking me home, and then you're going home, too, right?"

"Then I'm coming back to finish the flowers."

"Then I'm not leaving."

"Of course you are, Dottie. All you're doing is sleeping anyway."

"I was not sleeping. I was resting my eyes, and if you'd wanted help, you should have asked."

"I don't want help. I want you to go home and get some sleep."

"Well, you're just going to have to keep on wanting, then, because I'm not going!"

"Stop being so stubborn!"

"Stop being so irresponsible!"

"What's irresponsible about trying to get my job done?"

"Nothing, unless it's going to get you killed!"

"You might both want to stop shouting. I could hear you outside." The deep voice cut through their argument, and Shelby whirled, her heart racing.

"Do you have to keep doing that, Ryder?" she asked, and he raised an eyebrow.

"What?"

"Scaring years off my life. At the rate I'm aging, I might not make it to my thirtieth birthday."

"No need to worry about that, girl. You're not going to make it to tomorrow if you keep acting like a fool," Dottie muttered.

"What are you doing here, Ryder?" Shelby asked, completing ignoring Dottie's words and her dark look.

"I came back to escort you home. I would have been here sooner, but I had some business I needed to take care of."

"Business that includes the laptop your employee was looking at?"

"You really are persistent, Shelby Ann. You're right. It did include that."

"What information did he find?"

"I've got a man outside ready to give you a ride home, Dottie. I'll stick around here and keep an eye on Shelby Ann, make sure she gets home safely." He completely ignored the question, taking Dottie's frail arm and leading her from the kitchen.

She went without a fuss, her shuffling footsteps worrying Shelby. Dottie might be ornery, but she was family, and Shelby loved her. If anything happened to her—

She refused to even think about it.

Ryder opened the front door, the sound of traffic and Dottie's grousing drifting back to the kitchen.

"You'd better follow through on your promise, young man. If you don't, I know people. I'd hate to sic them on you, but I will," Dottie said, and Ryder mumbled something Shelby couldn't hear.

The door closed, silence fell.

Good. That's exactly what Shelby wanted. Peace. Silence. To be alone with her tools and her gum paste and her thoughts.

She sat at the counter again, went back to shaping petal after petal, silence swirling around her, a living, breathing entity that should have comforted her.

She knew silence, after all.

Had lived alone since her mother, Laura Beth, had told her it was time to make a go of things. *You're eighteen, Shelby Ann. It's time to make your mark on the world. Try acting or modeling. You're not classically beautiful, but you've got something sweet and lovely that translates well into pictures.* That's what she'd said as she'd handed Shelby the key to a small apartment just off Rodeo Drive, her second husband hovering behind her.

Chad Mitchell had made serious money buying and selling real estate in Hollywood. He was a player. A risk taker. A womanizer. He was also handsome, charming, very, very rich and a decade younger than Laura Beth.

Shelby's older sister insisted that Laura had sen-

Shelby away so that she could maintain a facade of youth and keep her younger husband's interest. For years, Shelby had refused to believe it, but the older she got, the more she observed her mother's fly-by-night attitude and the easier it was to think her sister might have been right.

She sighed, not sure why she was thinking about the past.

Maybe Dottie's mention of Beulah had sparked it.

Beulah had loved unconditionally with the kind of scriptural love that Shelby was always striving for. Selfless. Sacrificing. She so wanted to live those things out in her life, but she also wanted to experience them. She wanted to know the beauty of being the recipient of that kind of love.

She'd spent years believing that God would grant her that desire, but His plans for her life had taken her in a different direction. No white picket fence. No kids playing in the yard. No husband to share life's burdens with. Just her work and her friends. It was enough. It had to be.

She was blessed, and she had no right to complain. Sure, she was going through a rough patch in her personal life, in *every part of her life,* but God would bring her through it just as He always did.

She might not have had a traditional childhood, but Beulah had insisted on church every Sunday morning when she was around, and Shelby had continued to attend when she wasn't, forging a faith that neither her mother nor her sister had understood.

Beulah had understood, though, and she'd encouraged Shelby to seek God's will for her life, cheering her on when she'd signed up for culinary school, offering her a loan when she'd decided to open a bakery, suggesting Spokane, Washington, as the perfect place to do it.

There Shelby was, in her successful bakery, a tray full of orchids beside her, her life full and somehow empty all at the same time.

She stood, trying to ease the cramp in her back. The muscles knotted, pulling so tight she couldn't breathe or move or even think. She grabbed the counter, cold sweat beading her brow, her breath coming in short, shallow gasps because deeper ones hurt too much.

"What's wrong?" Ryder stepped into the kitchen, and Shelby shook her head, because it was all she could manage.

"Try to relax." His palms smoothed down her back, his fingers light as they probed, found the seized muscles near her incision.

"Don't—"

But he'd already started kneading the spot, the pain increasing for a split second before it eased, his touch like liquid fire, melting tension.

Melting Shelby.

She shivered, tried to move away.

"Let me finish. If I don't, the muscles will seize

again," he said, his gruff voice raking along her nerves, bringing them all to attention, and she knew she was so close to falling, she wasn't sure she was even still standing on the edge.

She shifted again, trying to move away from his touch. "Ryder—"

"That guy you saw on the laptop at your place? He hacked into the mainframe of the sheriff's department. The sheriff is worried that information has been leaking out, and he's hoping it's not leaking out of one of his men. He asked me to try to infiltrate the system, look up information about a case that's been open for nearly a decade, because he wanted to see how easy it would be for someone else to get in. My man was able to do it with no trouble at all," he said, his fingers and palms kneading and working.

"How is that connected to Maureen or me?" she asked, her words sluggish. She felt drugged, her muscles loose and warm. If she hadn't been standing, she might have closed her eyes and fallen asleep.

"The open case revolved around a serial arsonist who's been working in Washington. He's taken out several businesses in Seattle and Spokane, burned down a private school in Olympia. State police have connected him to at least a dozen fires statewide. His M.O. matches the one used at Maureen's place. Only, no one has ever been hurt before. The sheriff isn't sure if someone leaked information about the case or if the guy who killed Maureen is the arsonist."

"You could have told me all that earlier," she said as his hands slid to her shoulders, found the sore muscles in her neck.

"Client confidentiality, Shelby Ann. There are always going to be things I can't tell you about my work, but the sheriff asked me to share the information with you. He wants to keep you updated on the case, and he also wants to know if Maureen was working the serial-arsonist angle for a book."

"She never mentioned it."

"There's one more thing." His thumbs smoothed circles at the base of her neck, and she felt so limp, so liquidy she wasn't even sure she cared what else he had to say.

"What?"

"While I was at the sheriff's office, Hunter Lewis was brought in for questioning."

"Maureen's son?"

"He was in town the morning she died. Flew in the night before. Supposedly to surprise her on her birthday."

"That doesn't mean he's a murderer. Besides, the guy I saw didn't look like Maureen's son."

"The sheriff thinks it's possible he hired someone to murder Maureen."

"What? No way. They weren't close, but Maureen loved her son." Shock poured ice water into

Shelby's veins, and she turned, found herself face to chest with Ryder.

She looked up into his dark chocolate eyes, got caught in the heat of his gaze. Her heart jumped, her pulse leaped, her palms itched to touch his razor-stubble-covered jaw.

She clenched her fist, stepped back, bumping into the counter.

"Careful," he said, his hands cupping her waist and staying there. "Maureen was worth a lot of money, Shelby, and money can bring out the worst in people. Even family. Sometimes, especially family. I'm planning to go to his hotel and have a talk with Hunter. I thought you'd like to come along."

She did not want to spend another minute with Ryder and his magical hands.

"I have to finish these flowers. They still need to be painted."

"I can think of better uses of your time." His gaze dropped to her lips, and something unfurled in Shelby's belly, begged her to lean just a little closer, stretch up on her toes, do something much, much more interesting than painting flowers.

"Ryder—"

"What are you afraid of, Shelby Ann? Me?" he asked, his finger trailing up her arm, resting in the hollow of her throat, measuring her fear in the frantic racing of her pulse.

Only it wasn't just fear that had her pulse racing.

It was Ryder and everything he represented.

All the things she'd prayed for so long for and had finally, *finally* given up on.

All the things her family had scoffed at, but that Shelby had wanted so desperately to find.

Love.

Forever.

Happiness in the arms of someone who loved her just the way she was.

She blinked back hot tears, slipping from Ryder's embrace.

"I think I would like to go see Hunter, after all," she said and then did the only thing she could think of that wouldn't lead to heartache.

She turned and ran from the kitchen.

ELEVEN

Ryder followed Shelby, slamming his hand on the door before she could open it.

"You're running away," he said, his body still humming with a need he wouldn't give in to, his hands itching to smooth the frown line from between her brows, trace the line of her jaw, cup the silky, smooth skin of her neck.

"And?"

"You don't need to. I'm not going to take something you don't want to give," he responded, forcing his voice to stay light, his breathing to remain even.

"That's the problem, Ryder. I *want* to give it." She brushed a lock of dark hair from her cheek, her hand shaking, her eyes darkly shadowed.

"Then what are you afraid of?"

"Being disappointed again. I have a track record, Ryder. Two strikes, and I'm out of the relationship game. Come on. I still have work to do tonight, and it's not getting done while we're standing here talking." She put her hand on the door handle, and he covered it with his, stopping her before she could walk outside.

"Maybe that's the problem, Shelby Ann."

"What?"

"You've been with people who make relationships into games. They're not."

"Right. Good point. Now, I really want to get out of here, because—"

"Chicken." He cut her off.

"So what if I am? We have bigger things to worry about. Like finding out if Hunter Lewis killed his mother and is trying to kill me."

"You weren't in such a hurry to do that five minutes ago."

"We've already established that I'm a chicken, Ryder. I'm also hungry, tired and just want to forget everything for a while. Make the cake for the wedding tomorrow night and pretend that things are just like they've always been, but I can't, so I'm coming to the hotel with you. Now, can we please go?" Her voice shook, and she looked as if she was on the verge of tears. He nodded, tugging her away from the door.

"Let me go first."

"So you can get shot instead of me?"

"If it comes to that, yes."

"No."

"It's my job to keep you safe, Shelby Ann."

"It's *my* job to keep me safe," she responded, standing as tall as her five-four frame would allow.

"Take it up with Dottie. She's the one who hired me and made me promise to guard you with my life."

"What?"

"Dottie hired me to be your bodyguard." For the price of two doughnuts a day for life, but Shelby didn't need to know that.

"I need to have a talk with that woman," Shelby muttered, her cheeks flushed pink. "But before I do, I'm *un*hiring you."

"Sorry. Once I accept a client, that client is the only one who can terminate my services. Stay here. I need to make sure the area is clear."

He opened the door, motioning for Shelby to stay back as he surveyed the area. Dusk had fallen, casting long shadows across the pavement, but there was no sign of danger. Nothing to indicate they were being watched.

He signaled for Shelby to follow, shielding her with his body as she locked the door, her shoulders stiff.

"There's no need to be a sore loser."

"I'm too terrified to be a sore anything."

"There's no need to be scared. I'll protect you with my life."

"That's why I'm scared," she mumbled as he helped her into the Hummer.

"I can take care of both of us, okay? Everything is going to be fine." He skimmed a knuckle down her jaw, then forced himself to step away. She tempted him in a way he hadn't been tempted in a long time, but he couldn't afford to be distracted.

He hopped into the Hummer and started the engine, glancing her way when Shelby's stomach growled. "Hungry?"

"Seeing as how my stomach has already made the announcement, I guess it wouldn't do any good to deny it," she responded with a half smile that show-cased her dimple and the pouty fullness of her lips.

"We can stop for burgers on our way to the hotel."

"A salad will be fine," she said as he pulled into a fast-food drive-through.

"You haven't eaten all day. You need more than salad." He ordered two cheeseburgers, a large French fries and a milkshake, handing Shelby the bag as he pulled away from the window.

Much as he would have liked to bring her for a real meal of decent food, they didn't have time. Hunter was expecting them, and Ryder had a feeling that he wouldn't wait around if they weren't on time.

"Go ahead and eat what you want. I'll take what's left."

"You know what, Ryder? You make it really hard not to like you." She sighed, pulling out a fry and biting into it.

"Is there a reason why you don't want to like me?"

"*A* reason? There are a million reasons, but it's already too late. I like you, and there doesn't seem to be a whole lot I can do about it." She handed him a burger half-unwrapped for easy eating. Typical Shelby, taking care of someone else before she took care of herself.

It was time for someone to take care of her, and Ryder figured that someone might as well be him.

He bit into the burger, gestured to the bag. "One fry isn't enough. Keep eating. You need the calories."

"Keep sweet-talking me, Ryder. I like it." She pulled the second burger from the bag. "Do you think Hunter will give us any information that will help us figure out who Maureen's murderer is?"

"I don't think he'll say much. The only reason he agreed to meet with me was because I was there the morning of the explosion. He wants to pick my brain as much as I want to pick his. Having you there will be a bonus for him."

"I don't think he hired someone to kill his mother. If he did, why would he show up in Spokane the night before she was murdered?" Shelby said, passing Ryder a fry.

"Good question. One I'm sure the sheriff's department has an answer for."

"The sheriff didn't say?"

"He's not saying much about possible suspects or motives, but he did mention the Good Samaritan murders again. I'm planning to take a trip out to the state prison tomorrow to visit Catherine Miller. See what she has to say."

"Good idea. I know Maureen visited her several times last month. She was really excited about the story. *Angel of Darkness: Murders at Good Samaritan.* That's what she planned to call the book. She thought it was going to be her bestseller yet," Shelby said, tossing her half-eaten burger into the empty bag.

"Finish that up. You need the—"

"Calories? So you said, but I'm not hungry anymore." She sighed.

"Starving yourself won't bring Maureen back, and it won't solve her murder."

"I'm not starving myself. I'm just too sick to eat."

"Sick?" He pulled into Davenport Hotel parking garage, taking three spaces near the hotel lobby entrance, the Hummer angled so Shelby could exit close to the door.

"Not *sick* sick. Just…sorry that Maureen didn't get a chance to finish the book."

"That's the thing about life, Shelby Ann. We never know how long we've got, so we have to live it the best way we can every day," he said gently, brushing a stray curl from her cheek, his fingers lingering on her smooth skin.

She was definitely a temptation, but he had a job to do, a man to interview, and he couldn't let himself be distracted by Shelby.

"I'm coming around to your side. Don't get out of the Hummer until I give you the all clear." He got out before she could argue, rounding the

Hummer quickly as he scanned the parking area. A few patrons walked between the cars, talking quietly, completely caught up in their worlds and their lives, completely unaware that a murderer could be nearby.

Ryder was acutely aware of the fact.

Acutely aware of every person, every corner, every dark shadow. Even before Dottie had hired him, he'd been determined to protect Shelby. Now doing so was his job, his mission, and he didn't take that lightly.

But there was something else building between them, and it couldn't be denied any more than the danger that stalked Shelby could be.

The time to explore it would come. Eventually.

For now, he had to keep doing what he'd been doing, focusing his energy on keeping Shelby safe.

State-of-the-art security system in place.

A team of operatives ready to provide 24/7 protection.

All the tools Ryder had available thrown into the mix.

He hoped it would be enough.

Prayed it would be.

He opened the Hummer door, ushering Shelby into the Davenport.

Shelby tried to keep pace with Ryder's long-legged stride, but she nearly tripped as they stepped across the threshold and into the Davenport's posh lobby. He didn't miss a step, his arm sliding around her waist, supporting her weight as he continued to walk.

She tried to move away, but he didn't release his hold, and struggling would only make a scene.

Not that they hadn't already done that.

Walking around with Ryder was like walking around wearing a giant placard that read Stare at Me.

Or maybe Stare at the Guy I'm With.

When Ryder was around, people noticed.

Not that Shelby cared much about that.

She'd spent her childhood walking in the shadow of her mother and sister. Both breathtakingly beautiful, charming and more self-absorbed than either was likely to admit.

Shelby loved them anyway.

She wouldn't love a guy *like* them, though.

She preferred men like Andrew. Good-looking in an understated way. More likely to blend in than to stand out. Unobtrusive but still confident.

Sneaky.

Two-timing.

Untrustworthy.

Being understated and unobtrusive hadn't kept Andrew from being those things. Nor had it kept him from being self-absorbed, selfish and self-serving. Shelby was happy to be rid of him. She only wished she'd kept the ostentatious diamond ring he'd given her when he'd proposed as a reminder of just how foolish she'd been. The ring hadn't been her style at all, but he'd been so proud of the large, gaudy diamond, insisting that it suited her.

Her first hint that his solicitous concern and eagerness to listen was nothing more than a well-staged act in a play he was creating.

Shelby would have preferred something less traditional.

Maybe a sapphire or ruby ring.

If Andrew had been listening to anything she'd said in the months leading up to their engagement, he would have known that. She'd accepted the ring anyway. Worn it for five months, feeling it like a lead weight on her finger.

Still, she'd worn it.

Until Andrew hadn't shown up for a friend's wedding, and Shelby had gone looking for him.

She'd wanted the dream so badly that she'd been willing to ignore the subtle signs that Andrew wasn't the man she'd thought, but she hadn't been able to ignore seeing him exchanging a long, passionate kiss with the Realtor who was listing his apartment.

She frowned as Ryder hurried her to the elevator, a gaggle of women whispering and pointing as they passed.

"Could they be any more obvious?" she said under her breath, and Ryder smiled.

"Jealous?"

"Hardly." She stepped onto the elevator, Ryder's hand firm against the small of her back. Making good choices in men wasn't high on the list of things she did well. As a matter of fact, she was pretty sure it was right there at the bottom. So, if she wanted to trust Ryder, if she wanted to lean on him, it was probably a mistake, and she most definitely should *not* give in to the urge.

Which was okay, because she was done with men. D.O.N.E.

Done.

"You look upset. Are you sure you're up to this?" Ryder asked as the elevator doors opened onto the third floor.

"Yes. I'm just not sure Hunter is going to be happy to see us. Did you call ahead?"

"I arranged everything, and we're right on time for the meeting I set up with him. But that's not really why you're upset, is it?" He stopped walking, tugging at her apron strings to pull her back.

"Will you please stop tugging at my apron every time you want to stop me?" she asked.

"You're awfully touchy all of the sudden, Shelby Ann."

"Because I don't want to play games that I'm bound to lose."

He sobered at that, releasing his hold, but moving toward her, graceful and muscular as a jungle cat.

She shivered, but didn't back up.

Give a man an inch, and he'd take a million miles.

Another Beulah truism, but Shelby wasn't afraid of Ryder taking more than she gave. She was scared to death of handing it to him. Every inch, every mile of her foolish, fickle emotions, dreams, hopes.

"I already told you that relationships aren't games," he said quietly. Shelby nodded, because she was afraid of what she might say if she opened her mouth.

"Shelby Simons? Is that you?" The high-pitched, almost childlike voice could only belong to one person.

The one person Shelby most did *not* want to see.

She turned anyway, nearly flinching as she met Stephanie Parsons's perfectly made-up eyes and saw Andrew standing a few steps behind her.

Okay. So, *he* was the person Shelby most didn't want to see, but Stephanie was a close second.

"Hey, how are you, Stephanie? Andrew?" She smiled, but ice flowed into her heart. She might not want Andrew, might not care about him, but that didn't mean she wanted to see him at a hotel with his new girlfriend.

"How are we? We're wonderful, aren't we, dear?" Stephanie patted Andrew's arm, a huge diamond flashing on her left ring finger.

Oh, no.

No, no, no!

Andrew had *not* proposed and given her the exact ring he'd given Shelby!

Of course the scoundrel had.

"Better than wonderful. We're getting married next spring. We're here checking out the ballroom and reception area at the hotel. It's gorgeous. Just gorgeous," Stephanie continued, and Shelby wanted to gag.

"I'm sure it will be the perfect venue. If you two will excuse me, we have an appo—"

"Don't rush off just yet, Shel. We were planning to stop by your bakery earlier today to ask you a question, but didn't have the time." Andrew grabbed her hand, his palm soft and clammy and slightly disgusting.

She frowned, stepping back and bumping into the solid wall of Ryder's chest. Nothing soft or clammy or disgusting about him.

"What question?" It had better not be *Will you make the cake for our wedding?* Because if it was, Shelby couldn't be held responsible for her actions.

"We were hoping you'd make the cake for our wedding."

"You're kidding, right?"

"Why would I be? We're exes, but we're also friends, and you're the best baker in town. Stephanie and I want the best for our big day."

"We *aren't* friends, Andrew."

"Of course we are."

"No. We. Are. Not," she annunciated, but he still didn't get it.

"I know you're hurt, but try to put that aside and share this special time with us."

"I'll give you special." She attempted to lunge at

them, but Ryder grabbed her apron tie again, and she boomeranged right back into his chest.

"She can't make the cake." Ryder cut in and Andrew frowned, his eyes flashing with impatience.

"And you are?"

"Ryder."

"Well, Ryder, I don't want to be rude—"

"I'm afraid I don't feel the same way. As a matter of fact, I'm more than happy to be rude. Come on. Let's go, Shelby Ann." He started walking, and Shelby hurried to follow.

"This will only take a minute. We just—"

Ryder knocked on a door, completely ignoring Andrew's sputtered protest as it opened and Maureen's son appeared.

Tall and handsome with pitch-black hair and sky-blue eyes, Hunter Lewis studied them dispassionately, light purple dress shirt wrinkled, his chin covered with stubble.

"You're Ryder, right? And you're Shelby Simons. I recognize you from some pictures Mom posted to her website. Best cheese Danishes in town, right?"

"That's right."

"Come on in. I'm sorry that our meeting will have to be quick. The sheriff asked me to take a polygraph test in an hour. My lawyer suggested I comply."

"You didn't want to?" Ryder asked as they stepped into the room.

"I have a business to run in Chicago. It's not running itself while I'm gone. Drink?" He lifted a decanter of amber liquid, setting it back down when they both declined.

"Yeah. Me, neither. Sad to say, alcohol won't fix my problems. So, you want to pick my brain about Mom, right? What do you want to know? If she was a good mother? If we got along? If I paid someone to murder her?" He directed the question at Ryder, but his gaze was on Shelby, his blue eyes seeming to be searching for something.

"I was wondering what you were doing in town the morning of her murder." Ryder didn't hold back, and Hunter shrugged.

"It was her birthday. I thought that was as good a time as any to try to mend fences with her. I guess I left it for too long."

"So, you *didn't* get along?"

"Is it possible to get along with someone who isn't around? Mom spent most of my childhood flying from city to city doing research for her books. When I was eighteen, she gave me fifty thousand dollars and told me to get an apartment and a car and find a job."

The story reminded Shelby of her own, and her heart went out to the young man Hunter must have been. Scared. On his own. No family to depend on.

"You did pretty well for yourself on that fifty thousand. You're CEO of a software company, living in a penthouse in Chicago's business district and earning a six-figure salary. Not bad for a kid who was kicked to the curb at eighteen."

"You've been doing your research, Ryder, and you're right. I did do just fine. I never took another dime from my mother, and I never planned to. Like I told the police, I don't need her money. Even if I did, I'd have rather begged on the street than ask for it. If they want a murder suspect, they're going to have to look somewhere else."

"Where else do you think they should look?" Ryder seemed completely relaxed, but Shelby could almost feel the energy humming through him.

"Back four years. The police need to reopen the Dark Angel case. If they find the real Good Samaritan murderer, they'll find the person who killed my mother."

"The murderer is in jail," Shelby said, and Hunter speared her with a hard look.

"Is she? Mom called me up a couple of days ago, almost manic with excitement. She was convinced a murderer was still on the loose, and she said she was going to prove it. I laughed. Told her there was no way she was going to be able to prove that a guilty woman was innocent. We argued, and she ended up hanging up on me. If you want to know the truth, that's why I decided to come out for her birthday. I felt guilty for upsetting her. Now, if you'll excuse me, I need to get ready for my polygraph test." He opened the door, tension oozing out of him as he waited for them to leave.

"I'm really sorry for your loss, Hunter," Shelby offered, and he nodded.

"Thanks. Mom was a huge fan of your bakery, and I'm sorry that you had to be dragged into this mess. My mother was self-absorbed, but I know she wouldn't have wanted to cause you any trouble." He smiled, his face changing from somber and slightly angry to handsome and charming. A chameleon, but was he a killer?

Shelby didn't think so.

Then again, she hadn't thought Andrew was a lying, cheating creep, either.

She hadn't thought Andrew would kiss her best friend while wearing the tux he was supposed to marry Shelby in.

She hadn't thought either of those things, but they'd been true.

Going with her feelings wasn't a good idea.

She's proven that over and over again, but the thought of Hunter killing his mother just didn't seem to fit with what she knew about Maureen's life.

She sighed, following Ryder down the hall as the door clicked softly behind her.

TWELVE

"What do you think?" Ryder asked as he pushed the elevator button for the lobby.

"About Hunter?" Shelby asked, because she wasn't sure how to answer.

Maybe she wasn't the best judge of character, but she really didn't think Hunter had hired someone to kill Maureen. Still, saying it felt wrong. As if by giving her opinion, she might prove the opposite to be true.

Wasn't that how it always happened with her?

As soon as she decided someone was worth trusting, she was proven wrong.

"Who else? Did he plan his mother's murder and come here to try to throw the police off his scent? Or is he as innocent as he says? Come on, Shelby Ann. I know you have an opinion. Share it."

"Innocent," she said, because she couldn't seem to deny Ryder anything.

Which was another problem altogether.

"That's what I think."

"Really?" she asked as the elevator doors swung

open, and Ryder pressed a hand to her back, urging her into the lobby.

She went reluctantly, bracing herself for what she knew she'd see.

There was no way Andrew had left without asking her about the cake again.

He wasn't the kind of person to give up that easily, and Shelby was sure he was lying in wait somewhere, probably smooching his fiancée.

A sight she definitely did not want to see again.

"The way I see things, Hunter would have to be a fool to have come here to throw the police off his scent. He's not a fool," Ryder continued, apparently oblivious to her tension.

Why shouldn't he be?

She shouldn't *be* tense.

Not about seeing a man she didn't love with a woman she didn't like.

"What's wrong?" he said, proving that he sensed more than she wanted him to.

"Nothing."

"Something."

"Okay. You want to know the truth? I'm sure Andrew is still lurking around here somewhere, and I'm not happy about it."

"Andrew the ex with the Barbie-doll fiancée? Why do you care if he's here?"

"Because he's going to ask me about the cake again, and he's going to keep asking."

"So, just keep saying no."

"You make it sound so easy."

"It is."

"No. It's not." She rounded on him, looking into his dark eyes and almost losing her train of thought, because maybe he was right. Maybe it really was that easy.

"Why not? He's your ex. He doesn't have any power over you."

"Of course he does. He was the last straw, Ryder. He proved what I didn't want to believe, and now he expects me to pretend he did me a favor."

"Don't." He touched her cheek, wiping away a tear she hadn't even realized had fallen.

"Pretend he owes me a favor? I don't plan to."

"No, Shelby Ann. Don't cry over someone who isn't worth it."

"I'm not. I'm crying for what he represented and what I'm never going to have. Dreams and forever and all that stuff my mother and grandmother and sister insisted I'd never find. I guess they were right."

"Maybe not," he said, his gaze lifting, his eyes focused on something just behind her.

"They're there, aren't they?" She started to turn, but Ryder wound an arm around her waist, his hand skimming across her lower spine and hooking in her apron tie.

"Don't turn around, Shelby Ann. Don't let them know you know they're watching."

"I don't care if they know, and Andrew is going to come over here whether I acknowledge him or not."

"Let him come, then." Ryder's lips brushed her ear, his rough whisper raking along her nerves, bringing every one of them to life.

"What are you doing?" she asked, her heart thundering in her ears, her body soft with longing for whatever it was he had planned.

Stupid, stupid, stupid.

But she couldn't seem to step away.

"Just a little evasive action. Nothing to be worried about." He tugged her into a cozy alcove, tracked tiny kisses along the line of her jaw, stopping at the corner of her mouth, his dark eyes staring into hers, all his amusement gone.

"Ryder—"

"Do you want me to stop?"

Did she?

"Do you?" he repeated, and she nodded her head while her foolish arms wrapped around his neck and pulled him closer.

So close.

Their lips touched, light, easy, but she felt the kiss more than she'd ever felt anything else. Felt it swirling through her, stealing away all her worries and fears and doubts.

Andrew didn't exist.

Stephanie didn't exist.

Hunter didn't exist.

The lobby, the people, the reality of where she was and who she was with and what she should *not* be doing didn't exist.

All that existed was that moment, that light touch of lips.

She sighed, pulled him even closer, let herself get lost in the moment.

"Really, Shelby. Is this the place for that kind of display?" Andrew's voice was like a splash of ice water, bringing Shelby to full awareness again.

She jumped back, her chest heaving, heart pounding, lips burning.

Ryder's kiss still swirling through her.

"She's not baking that cake for you, Andrew, so beat it," Ryder growled, his voice hard and just slightly uneven.

"I'll let Shelby tell me that."

Shelby tried to turn to face Andrew, to tell him what he claimed he needed to hear, but Ryder caught her jaw in his broad hand, his touch as gentle as a summer breeze, and kissed her again.

Kissed her as if he meant it.

Kissed her as if she'd never been kissed before.

Kissed her until she forgot all about Andrew and weddings and cakes and two strikes and being out.

She broke away, scared by the force of her emotions, scared of what she saw in his eyes. "You shouldn't have done that."

"I didn't. *We* did." He looked as shaken as she felt, and she wanted to deny that, deny the truth of his words.

But she couldn't.

Because *they* had kissed.

Right there in the lobby of the Davenport Hotel with a dozen people looking on.

With Andrew looking on.

A little evasive action had turned into something unexpectedly strong and real and undeniable.

She took a shaky breath, tried to clear her head, but it was impossible with Ryder watching so intently.

"We need to go. I've got work to do at the bakery. A wedding tomorrow night, and those flowers have to be done. I—"

"Stop," he said quietly, and she did, blinking back more of the tears that been falling since the day Maureen died.

"I can't do this, Ryder."

"You don't have to do anything."

"But I already did."

"It was just a kiss, Shelby Ann. It doesn't have to mean forever," he said gently, hooking a strand of hair behind her ear, his fingers searing her skin.

"But it could be?" she asked, the question slipping out before she could stop it.

"If you want it to."

"Don't say that."

"You asked."

"But I didn't really want to know the answer."

"Too late," he said, and she couldn't look in his eyes anymore, couldn't stand there listening to his deep voice and his easy words.

Couldn't, so she ran from him for the second time in twenty-four hours, her heart shouting *coward* as she beelined for the door.

Ryder barely managed to snag the back of Shelby's apron before she made it out the door. Slow and sluggish, his mind and body still wrapped up in the feel of her lips, the silkiness of her hair, he'd almost let her walk outside ahead of him.

Almost.

He'd meant to keep the kiss friendly and light. Meant to do nothing more than show Andrew and his insipid fiancée how little Shelby cared about their wedding, their cake, their presence.

He'd made an error of calculation.

Hadn't factored in just how deeply the kiss would affect him.

He wouldn't make another one.

"I really have to stop wearing this apron," Shelby muttered as he pulled her to a stop.

"That would be a shame, Shelby Ann, since it gives me something to grab on to when you're trying to run from me."

"I'm not running," she said, and he raised an eyebrow, waiting for the truth.

"Okay," she admitted. "So I *am* running, but I still need to stop wearing this, because I really do need to go back to the bakery, and you stopping me every five seconds isn't getting me there."

"This time I stopped you because I need to walk outside first."

"Right. While I stand here waiting for you to make the ultimate sacrifice."

"No need for dramatics. Just stay here until I signal for you to follow," he said, purposely trying to ruffle her feathers. Better to have her angry and spewing fire than embarrassed and shut down.

"I am not being drama—"

He walked outside, cool air bathing his heated skin and cooling his fevered blood.

Focus.

That's what he needed to keep Shelby safe.

Not kisses in hotel lobbies.

But he couldn't deny he'd enjoyed it.

Couldn't deny that he'd meant what he'd said.

One kiss could lead to forever if he and Shelby let it.

Sunset painted the sky in shades of gold and purple and cast long shadows across the parking lot. People strolled along the sidewalk, the busy shopping district sparkling in the dusky light. Not a good time of day to be out. Too many people. Too many shadows. Ryder scanned the area, searching for signs of trouble before gesturing for Shelby to follow him outside.

He hurried Shelby into the Hummer, closing the door quickly. She wanted to go back to the bakery to work for a few hours, and that was fine by him, but he had no intention of leaving her there alone. Even with a new alarm system and security cameras installed, she wouldn't be safe until the guy who was after her was behind bars.

He pulled out his cell phone, dialing a navy buddy who worked for the state police.

"Delaney, here. What's up?" Tyson Delaney grumbled, and Ryder imagined him pouring over a cold case, searching for new leads. As a detective with the Washington State Police, he had a reputation for solving cases others couldn't. The job kept him working late and running full tilt, which was probably how Tyson wanted it.

"You set up that appointment with Catherine Miller for me?" Ryder asked, knowing his friend had. When Tyson said he was going to do something, he followed through.

"Tomorrow morning at nine. I went and visited her myself a few minutes ago. The Spokane County deputy sheriff was walking out as I was walking in. Miller wasn't happy about so many visitors, and she refused to answer my questions."

"Hopefully, she'll be in a better frame of mind in the morning."

"Don't count on it, friend."

"I'll try not to," he glanced at Shelby, but she was staring out the window, probably trying hard to pretend she wasn't listening. "One more thing, Ty.

What do you know about the serial arsonist who's been working in the area?"

"I know I was assigned the case six months ago, and I haven't found one new lead, and I know that the Spokane County Sheriff's Department just sent me information about the explosion that killed Maureen Lewis. I'm hoping I'll find a fresh lead there."

"You think the cases are connected?"

"The sheriff does, so it's worth looking into. I've got a dinner engagement in ten, so I need to go. Call me if you have any trouble getting in to see Miller."

"Will do." He hung up, pulling up next to Old Blue, the bakery dark and untouched.

"Thanks for dropping me off, Ryder," Shelby said as if he were going to let her out of the Hummer and leave her there.

"Who said anything about dropping you off?"

"Me. I need some...space."

"Because of the kiss?" he asked, and she shrugged. "Maybe."

"Tell you what, you can have all the space you need after we catch the guy who's trying to kill you. Stay here until I come for you. The less time you spend out in the open, the happier I'll be." He got out of the Hummer, not waiting for her response. In this instance, her need for space was superseded by the safety plan he'd put into place. He used the spare key to open the bakery, turning off the alarm before walking back to the Hummer. "Ready?"

"No." But she got out of the Hummer anyway,

marching into the bakery and straight to the kitchen without saying another word.

"You're upset, Shelby, but this is what I have to do to keep you safe," he said as she opened edible paint and began dabbing yellow onto a flower.

"I keep telling you that *I* have to keep me safe. Not you. Not Dottie. Not anyone else." She dropped the flower onto a tray, grabbed another one.

"You're keeping yourself safe by letting experts help you."

"I don't want help. I want…silence." She painted another flower, her head bent, dark curls falling across her cheek and hiding her expression.

"Okay."

"No. It isn't okay, Ryder, because you're standing half a foot away, all big muscles and dark eyes and dependability, and I'm thinking about heroes and forevers and a dozen things I shouldn't be. Silence isn't going to change that any more than going back and undoing our kiss would." She sighed, setting the tiny paintbrush down.

"Two kisses," he corrected.

"I don't need a reminder."

"Neither do I, but like I told you before, I'm not going to take something you don't want to give. Those kisses can be nothing, Shelby Ann, or they can be a whole lot. It all depends on you." He looked deep into sky-blue eyes.

"That's the problem, Ryder. I want too much, and every time I think I've found it, it all falls apart."

"Wanting love isn't too much, Shelby. Wanting forever isn't."

"For me, it is. Before I got blown off my feet and into your arms, I was content to become the neighborhood cat lady."

"You don't have any cats."

"That's not the point. I broke up with Andrew, and I made peace with the fact that he was it. My last hurrah. I don't want to go back to wanting something I can't have."

"Shelby—"

"God puts us all on different paths, Ryder. This is mine." She gestured to the bakery. "My bakery, my friends, my family. I need to be content with that."

"You've forgotten something, Shelby Ann," he said quietly, and she met his eyes.

"What's that?"

"God puts us all on different paths, but sometimes people's paths converge, merge, become the same. When they do, He has a reason for it."

"I need to finish these flowers. How about we discuss this another time?"

"Fine. Let's talk about your work schedule instead."

"It's hanging on the wall in my office. Go ahead and take a look."

"Trying to get rid of me?"

"Yes." She placed another flower on the tray, smiling, and Ryder's gaze dropped to her lips, his thoughts skittering away so quickly he couldn't quite catch them again.

"Glad you're willing to admit it," he said, and then he turned and walked out of the kitchen, heading outside into the cool, crisp evening. He was leaving because if he stayed, he might give in to temptation and taste the sweetness of Shelby's smile, revisit those moments in the hotel lobby when all that had mattered was the yielding softness of her lips.

He leaned against the bakery's brick facade, getting ahold of himself as he rubbed the tight muscles of his thigh. Cars passed lazily, their drivers in no hurry to get wherever they were going. That seemed to be the pace of Spokane life. Slower than the big city he'd settled in after his injury. When he'd arrived in Washington State, he'd been sure he'd be bored within days, anxious to go back to New York and the frenetic pace of life there.

But he hadn't been bored.

Not even close.

He'd slipped into the slow pace of small-city living easily, let the distant white-tipped mountains and evergreen-topped hills soothe the still-raw edges of his emotions in a way New York City hadn't been able to. Still, he hadn't planned or expected to stay more than a year. He'd sublet his apartment with every intention of returning to it after twelve months.

He still planned to return, but the urgency he'd

felt when he'd left New York was gone. A few more weeks, a few more months, didn't seem like such a big thing.

As a matter of fact, when he looked into Shelby's eyes, he could imagine staying for a lot longer than that.

After he'd ended things with Danielle, he'd thought he was done with the dating scene, finished searching for a woman who obviously didn't exist. A woman who wanted the same things he did, who valued the same things he did. Not fame or fortune or excitement. Faith. Family. Forever. Home and hearth and all the things he'd longed for when he'd been lying in the hospital bed wondering if he'd ever walk again.

Shelby could be those things to him.

He could be those things to her.

He knew it deeply and with a certainty that left no room for doubt, but *she* doubted, and he wouldn't push her.

Because she was Shelby, and he cared too much.

He walked around the side of the building, checking the perimeter, but not expecting to find anything. The perp would be a fool to return, and Ryder didn't think he was that.

Behind the building, an alley yawned, dark and quiet and empty. Two Dumpsters. A stray cat. Probably a rat or two. Other than that, nothing.

The scent of decay hung heavy and cloying in cool night air, and bits of crime-scene tape still clung to the building. If he looked, would Ryder see Shelby's blood staining the pavement?

The image of her as she'd been in the hospital, vulnerable and scared, filled him with anger and the dark, hot need for retribution. The law's responsibility. God's responsibility, but that didn't mean Ryder couldn't play a part. He'd go to the prison, visit Catherine Miller, dig a little deeper into the case Maureen had been researching.

Maybe the answers they needed lay there.

One way or another, he planned to find out.

And he planned to keep Shelby safe.

Keep her alive.

Maybe even keep her close for a lot longer than the time it took to figure out who wanted her dead and why.

Hopefully, keep her close for a lot longer.

Time would tell.

Time and Shelby, because Ryder wouldn't push her, wouldn't demand anything she didn't want to give. He'd bide his time, wait her out, see what the future brought.

For now, he'd just keep following the path God had placed him on and trust that it would lead him to exactly the place he was supposed to be.

THIRTEEN

She walked across the meadow, a bouquet of pink peonies in her hand, the sun kissing her cheeks and heating her skin.

There.

Just up ahead.

He waited.

Back turned, hair gleaming in the sunlight. Her heart leaped in recognition, her body humming with love.

She wanted to call out to him, but a train rumbled past, the shriek of its horn loud enough to rip the flowers from her hand and send them skittering across the meadow. She ran to catch them, her feet sinking into a pile of crumbled cake and thick white frosting.

She fell, hands clawing at empty air, a woman's scream filling her ears, filling her head, spearing through her body until she wanted to join in with the endless shriek.

She jumped to her feet, looking for the man who'd waited.

Gone.

Ashes in the wind.

But he was there. Sunglasses down low on his nose, his cold blue eyes spearing into hers, pink peonies dripping with blood held out for her to take.

"No!" Shelby screamed, coming out of her bed as quickly as her drug-sluggish body could manage. Pain stole her breath, but she just kept going, racing to the bedroom door, a woman's screams still echoing in her head.

Screams and screams and more screams.

No. Not a woman.

An alarm.

She pivoted back to the bed, fumbled for the bedside light and turned it on, her brain refusing to process what the alarm meant. Fire? Intruder?

Alarm?

Alarm!

Ryder's team. He'd assured her that they were on the job. If the alarm went off, someone would be there within two minutes. Hunker down and wait it out. Those were Ryder's instructions when he'd walked her into the house, shown her how to set the alarm and reminded her not to set foot outside no matter what.

With the police running patrols on the quarter hour and the alarm set up, Shelby had been confident she'd have a good and safe night's sleep. So confident, she'd taken two of the pain pills.

Now she was going to pay for it, because the

alarm was still ringing, help hadn't arrived and her brain was working in slow motion, her panic muted and faraway.

Mazy cowered a few feet away, and Shelby scooped her up, stumbling toward the door again.

She stopped.

Was someone out there waiting for her to leave her room?

Was he?

The cold-eyed killer from her nightmare?

She backed away from the door, Mazy clutched close to her chest.

Two minutes.

That's what Ryder had said.

So where was help?

She didn't want to be shot again.

She didn't want to *die*.

So do something. Don't just stand here like a fool and wait to be attacked again!

No phone in her bedroom.

Cell phone downstairs in her purse.

Okay.

So, she'd lock the door and hunker down just like Ryder had told her to.

But two minutes had already come and gone, and the alarm still shrieked, and she was still alone. She needed another plan. A different one.

Get out of the house without being seen.

Out the window into the backyard.

It was the only way to avoid an intruder.

She locked the door, backed toward the window, expecting the old-fashioned crystal doorknob to explode and the door to open at any moment. Expecting *him* to be standing there, gun out, ready to finish what he'd started at the bakery.

Her stomach heaved at the thought, the pain medication she'd taken making her woozy and light-headed and sick.

And hot.

Really hot.

Not just hot, *roasting,* her drug-fogged brain insisting that she was about to fry like an egg on a hot rock.

She wrinkled her nose, inhaled. Coughed.

She didn't just feel as if she was cooking, she *smelled* as if she was cooking.

Smelled smoke. Saw it billowing up through the floorboards.

Fire!

The house burning around her, the alarm screaming, and Shelby cowering against a wall trying to decide if she should escape out the window.

Of course she should.

Now.

Before it was too late.

Open the window, hang from the sill, drop to the ground.

Easy as pie. Right?

Right.

"Please, God, let it be that easy," she prayed as

she tucked in her cotton pajama top, cinched the drawstring of her pants and shoved Mazy down the front of her shirt.

"Don't wiggle. I don't want you to fall."

She didn't want to fall, either.

But she'd rather fall than roast.

She unlocked the window and opened it, shoved out the screen. Looked down.

Why hadn't she bought a one-story rancher like her mother had suggested?

Why, oh why, oh why had she insisted on a two-story Tudor?

Heat seared the soles of her feet, and she knew she was out of time.

Up and over the windowsill, legs dangling, Mazy wiggling, fingers clutching wood as the alarm shrieked in her ears. Nothing between her and the ground but air.

Let go.

Just let go and drop.

She knew what she had to do, but her fingers wouldn't release their hold.

Let go!

Her back seized, the pain from her injury doing what her mind could not. Her grip loosened, and she fell so fast she didn't have time to brace for impact.

Feetfirst, tumbling back onto her butt and landing so hard the breath left her lungs. Up again, bare feet on cold grass as she ran toward the neighbor's house, pain searing through her, fear spurring her on.

A dark figure lunged from the shadows, and she screamed, Mazy barking hysterically as Shelby pivoted, tried to run away.

Too late.

Arms wrapped around her waist, viselike and hard, a voice shouting words she couldn't understand.

She screamed again, spinning around, Mazy howling, the alarm still shrieking.

"Get him, Mazy! Bite him!" she shouted, but the dog just burrowed deeper into her shirt.

"You don't really want her to bite me, do you?" Ryder growled close to her ear, the voice familiar as sunrise.

"Ryder!" She clutched his shirt, her hands fisted in soft cotton. "My house is on fire!"

"The fire department is already here. They should get things under control quickly. Come on. I want you out of this yard and out of the line of fire." He ushered her around the burning house, and she let him, because she didn't know what else to do.

The entire house was in flames, smoke billowing into the predawn sky, and she wasn't sure how it had happened or what she was supposed to do about it or even if she was really awake.

Maybe the fire, the alarm, the smoke were all part of some horrible dream.

Only, she could smell the smoke, see the flames, feel blisters forming on the bottom of her feet.

"My house," she whispered as Ryder helped her into the Hummer.

"It'll be okay," he responded, his palm resting against her cheek for a second before he turned to talk to a tall, dark-haired man.

One of his employees?

Probably, but Shelby didn't want to be introduced, didn't want to do anything but lean her head against the car's seat and close her eyes.

Mazy whined, wiggling out from under Shelby's pajamas and licking her cheek.

"It'll be okay." She repeated Ryder's words, but she wasn't sure she believed them.

Houses didn't suddenly burst into flames. Not the way hers had.

Someone had started the fire, and Shelby could have died in it.

"Ms. Simons?"

She opened her eyes, looked into the face of Fire Marshal Timothy Saddles. "It's bad, isn't it?" she asked, and he nodded.

"We should have it under control shortly, but the fire burned hot. Looks like it took out the entire lower level of the house. Do you have home owner's insurance?"

"Yes."

"You'll be able to recoup your losses, then, and you're alive. Things could be worse."

"I know."

"Did you hear anything before the fire began? See anything?"

"No. I'd only been home a couple of hours, and I was really tired. I took some pain medicine the doctor prescribed, and that's the last thing I remember until the fire alarm started shrieking."

"So, you didn't notice anything when you got home? No strange smells? No unfamiliar cars parked nearby."

"Ryder was with me. He checked everything out, and it was clear. Whoever set the fire did it while I was sleeping."

"The arsonist was fast and thorough, then. Knew what he was doing."

"What he was doing was trying to kill me. So, maybe he didn't know much, after all."

"Kill you or flush you out of the house. It's probably a good thing you went out the window rather than one of the doors. I'm going to talk to my crew. As soon as you know where you'll be staying, call me with your contact information."

"She'll be staying with me," Ryder said, stepping into sight, his blond hair mussed, his eyes flashing with anger.

"Do you have a card?" Saddles asked, and Ryder handed one to him.

"Call if you need to speak with Shelby, but she won't be going anywhere or speaking to anyone without me or one of my team members. You can run things through the receptionist at my office, and she'll make arrangements."

"That's—"

"How it's going to be, Chief. This is the second attack on Shelby's life. We can't afford for there to be another." He closed Shelby's door, blocking out the rest of the conversation, but not the sight of the still-smoldering Tudor.

Her house. Destroyed.

Everything she'd worked so hard for in ashes, and she wanted to be okay with it. Wanted to embrace the idea that she was alive and whole and healthy, and that everything that had been lost could be replaced.

Wanted to.

But she felt hollow and empty, her stomach twisting as firefighters continued to battle the blaze.

Maybe it was for the best. None of the dreams she'd put into the house had panned out. None of the hopes she'd set her heart on while she peeled old wallpaper and removed layers of paint from woodwork had come to fruition.

The driver's door opened, and Ryder got in, reaching for her before he spoke. Or maybe she was reaching for him, pulling herself toward his broad, strong chest, burying her face in the soft cotton of his shirt.

He smoothed her hair, murmured quiet words that said nothing and everything all at once.

It's okay.

You're okay.
Everything is going to be fine.

And somehow, despite the smoke and flames and frantic fire crew, despite her fear and worry, while Shelby leaned against Ryder's chest, inhaled his familiar scent, she could almost believe it was true.

FOURTEEN

They drove an hour to go five miles.

Shelby only knew that because she knew the area, recognized River Walk Plaza and the swank apartment buildings there.

She knew she should be thankful that Ryder had whisked her away from the charred remains of her house, from the endless questions of the sheriff, from the sympathetic but nosy stares of her neighbors, but all she felt was tired.

"Is this it?" she asked, as he pulled into a parking garage.

"Yes."

"You said it was a safe house. Not a swank apartment complex downtown."

"A safe house is anywhere that you're safe."

"I know. I just pictured an old farmhouse in the middle of a barren field. Somewhere out in the open with armed gunmen standing at every window, waiting to shoot intruders."

"You've watched too many movies, Shelby Ann. Come on. Let's get inside and get you settled. We have a few hours before our appointment with Catherine. You should be able to get some sleep before then."

"I'm not going to be able to sleep," she responded as he helped her out of the Hummer.

"We'll see."

"I won't." She lifted Mazy, and Ryder scooped the dog from her arms.

"I'm not sure my apartment manager will be happy about having a dog in the building, but we'll give it a try."

"*Your* apartment manager? I thought this was a safe house."

"It's my place and a safe house."

"Maybe this isn't such a good idea, Ryder." She dragged her sore, blistered feet. She hadn't mentioned the burns, but maybe she should. Maybe that would keep her from staying in Ryder's apartment.

With him.

"You were fine with it an hour ago."

"That was before I knew you were going to be staying in the *safe house* with me."

"You're making more of this than you need to. You're not the first client I've brought here, and you won't be the last," he said calmly, taking Shelby's arm and hurrying her to the building, keeping his body between her and the parking lot as they moved.

The 1920s facade opened into a three-story foyer and a wide marble staircase, the art-deco architecture speaking of bygone eras and attention to detail. Against one wall, a bank of elevators offered a quick ride to one of four stories, but Ryder led her to the stairs, ushering her up to the second floor, down a quiet hall and into a stairwell. Another two flights of stairs, and Shelby was panting, her back aching, her feet burning and bleeding.

"This is it, right?" she asked as he opened a door and led her out into another quiet hall.

"Almost."

"Almost? Where else is there to go?"

"I rent the loft."

"Loft? You mean penthouse?"

"I mean loft. Used to be the maintenance man's place back when this was a hotel, so it's more like an attic apartment than a penthouse. This way." His hand settled on her lower back, his fingers brushing her side as he steered her around a corner and to an unmarked door. He unlocked it, gestured for her to walk up a narrow flight of stairs.

A very narrow flight.

So narrow, her shoulders brushed against the walls. Her feet rubbed raw on the cement stairs, but she kept walking because if she stopped, Ryder would bump into her, and then she might turn around, throw herself into his arms and beg to be carried the rest of the way.

Finally, she reached another door, a small, locked metal box attached to the wall to one side of it.

"Hold on." Ryder reached around, his body

pressed close as he unlocked the box, punched a code into a keypad, then pushed the door open.

She stumbled into an oversize living area, anxious to be away from his heat and his scent and him.

Anxious to sit down, too, because her feet hurt, her back hurt, and if she thought about the embers of her house, she might just start crying.

"Glad you finally decided to show up," someone said, and Shelby whirled, her heart pounding as she stared into emerald-green eyes and a tan, handsome face.

"I took the long route. Just in case. Are we hooked into the building's security system?" Ryder responded as he closed the door, locking Shelby into the loft.

"Hooked in and functioning. We have a clear view of the exterior perimeter and the lobby." The man moved with lithe grace, his slender runner's build powerful beneath a white dress shirt and black slacks. A gun holster hugged his chest and side, the black handle of a gun brushing his arm as he walked out of a small galley kitchen and into the living room.

"Glad to hear it. Shelby, this is Darius Osborne. He'll be working security detail with me tonight. Darius. Shelby Simons."

"Nice to meet you, Shelby. Sorry it has to be under these circumstances." Darius shook her hand, his grip firm and strong, his gaze direct. Comforting. That's the vibe Shelby got from him, but she also sensed a dangerous edge beneath his vivid green eyes.

"Nice to meet you, too."

"You're probably exhausted. Why don't you settle in? Get some sleep?" He took her arm, moving her down a small hall as Ryder bent over a computer set up on the kitchen counter.

"I'm not really tired." She limped into the room he indicated, stepping back as he closed shades and blocked off her view of the brick side of another building.

"Ryder has the place set up for situations like this, so you'll be comfortable for however long you need to be here. Check in the dresser and closet for clean clothes. They might not fit well, but they'll be functional." He ignored her protest, walked through an open doorway and turned on a light. "There's a bathroom through there. If you need anything, just let me or Ryder know. We'll get it for you. No phone calls to friends, okay? No texting. No emailing. Nothing to give anyone any idea of where you are or who you're with."

"Like anyone would believe me if I told them," she said, and he frowned.

"You're in a very dangerous situation, Shelby. Someone wants you dead. If you want to stay alive, you'll do exactly what Ryder and I tell you to do. Go ahead and get some sleep." He walked out of the room, the soft click of the door sealing her in with Mazy and her thoughts.

Too many thoughts about too many things she had no control over.

As a matter of fact, it seemed she had no control over anything in her life lately. Not where she went, who she went with or what she did.

Be tough. Don't rely on anyone but yourself.

If her family had a motto, that would be it, and Shelby was trying really hard to live by it.

No more letting someone into her life. No more allowing another person to influence her decisions, determine her happiness.

No more putting her heart in someone else's hands.

Did putting her life in Ryder's hands count?

She sighed, limping across the room, the stench of smoke drifting around her, reminding her of the house she'd labored over, the dreams she'd built with every nail hammered, every wall painted.

Gone.

All of it.

She searched the closet and the drawers, found clothes in a variety of sizes, the tags still on all of them.

Darius was right.

Ryder *was* set up for this kind of thing.

Why wouldn't he be? He made a living protecting people.

She grabbed dark jeans and a T-shirt, took a quick shower in the white-tiled bathroom, washing away soot and smoke, cleaning her sore and blistered feet.

Wishing she could wash away her fear, clean away her worries just as easily.

God was in control.

He'd work things out for His best.

That was the truth of the situation, so there was no reason to fret or worry or wonder how she'd ever run a business from Ryder's safe house, or how Dottie and the four teens who relied on steady work and paychecks would fare if she had to close the doors for a few days.

No, she shouldn't worry and fret, but she *was* worried and fretting and upset, and no matter how much she didn't want them to, the tears she'd been pushing away slid down her cheeks as she towel-dried her hair and lay down on the bed.

What if she did have to close the bakery for a day or a week or a month?

Would she lose the bakery?

Would the people she cared about be forced back out on the street, begging for food and places to stay?"

And what about the house?

She had a mortgage to pay on the pile of ashes that remained. Ashes of the house and of the million dreams she'd built into it.

Dreams of a normal family with normal kids and a normal husband. Not the glamour and glitz and showiness of Shelby's childhood. Just a simple day-to-day routine, all of it lived out with a backdrop of love and acceptance.

A soft knock sounded on the door, and she ignored it, hoping that whoever it was would go away.

It had to be Ryder or Darius, and she wasn't up to facing either of them.

The door opened anyway, and she closed her eyes, pretending to sleep as someone walked across the room.

"I know you're awake," Ryder said, the mattress compressing as he sat on the edge of the bed.

"I'm trying not to be," she responded, opening her eyes as he touched her foot.

"You should have told me you were burned."

"It's not bad."

"It looks bad from where I'm sitting." He walked into the bathroom, came out a minute later with a first-aid kit. "This may hurt a little."

"Then don't do it."

"Sorry, Shelby Ann. I don't want you to get an infection." He rubbed antibiotic cream into the bottom of her foot, and she nearly jumped off the bed, pain shooting up her leg.

"That did *not* hurt *a little,*" she gasped, and he patted her shin.

"Sorry. The other one isn't as bad, so it shouldn't be as painful."

"I'll do it." She grabbed the ointment from his hand, sitting up cross-legged and examining her untreated foot. Two large blisters had popped and were oozing fluid, but things could have been worse.

She braced herself, smearing the ointment onto

the blisters and loosely covering both feet with gauze, Ryder's gaze steady, focused and *distracting*.

"It's been a rough night. How are you holding up?" He brushed hair from her forehead, his touch just as distracting as his gaze.

"I'm okay."

"Don't tell me what you think I want to hear. Tell me the truth," he said gently, and Shelby's throat tightened.

"If I tell you the truth, I'll start crying, and then I might never stop," she responded, because she couldn't look in his eyes and keep saying that she was fine, keep trying to hide what she really felt.

"Crying because of your house?" His fingers trailed down her cheek, skimmed down her arm until they were palm to palm.

"A little, but I'm more worried about the bakery. The people who work for me depend on it being open. If I can't be there, I'm not sure how long they can keep it running. I organize everything, prepare the orders for the day."

"You'll still be able to do that. This is our base camp, but it isn't the only place I can keep you safe. I'll take you back to the bakery tomorrow. I'll go with you while you deliver the wedding cake. Then we'll come back here, and I'll take you back to work the next day. Nothing will change."

"Everything has changed, Ryder," she said, because it had. Her life. Her business. Her home.

Her heart.

He'd changed it, made it yearn for him in a way she couldn't be comfortable with. Not if she was going to keep it whole and safe.

"It's going to be okay," he murmured, his lips brushing her forehead, and she closed her eyes, afraid he'd see how deeply his tenderness affected her.

"I'm really tired. I think I should try to sleep now." She moved away from his comforting touch and turned on her side, listening as he walked into the hall and closed the door.

A tear trickled down her cheek.

Then another and another until the pillow was soaked with them, her cheeks and neck soaked with them.

Shelby didn't bother wiping them away.

There was no one to see.

No one but God.

Shelby was sure He understood.

FIFTEEN

Dawn came early in Spokane, the sun rising in a blaze of yellow-gold light. Ryder watched it as he worked kinks out of his bad leg, the computer behind him, Darius leaning over it. Three hours of staring at the monitor, and Ryder had seen nothing. Not a bird. Not a dog. Not a person.

Too bad.

He'd been hoping the arsonist would show up looking for Shelby, hoping he'd have a chance to take the guy down and bring him in to the police.

He grimaced as he rubbed a knot from his thigh and eased into a stretch that would lengthen the muscles.

"What time are you taking off?" Darius asked, and Ryder glanced at the clock, sweat beading his brow as he slowly increased the stretch.

"Ten minutes."

"I'll let Shelby know," Darius offered, and if the client had been anyone other than Shelby, Ryder would have agreed. He had another five minutes of easy stretching and exercise to do before he started the day.

But the client *was* Shelby, and he had a personal interest in making sure she was okay, an interest that went far beyond protecting her.

"I'll get her." He stood, ignoring the sharp twinge in his leg.

"I knew you would."

"Meaning?"

"You have a lot more interest in her than you ever had in Danielle," Darius answered, his gaze still focused on the computer monitor, but Ryder knew his friend noticed every twitch, every nuance. It was what had made him a good SEAL, and what made him a good security contractor.

"Shelby is…different," he said truthfully.

"She's pretty, but not as beautiful as Danie—"

"Is there some reason why we're discussing this?"

"Just curious as to what you're thinking long-term."

"All I'm thinking about is keeping Shelby safe. Everything else will work itself out," Ryder responded, and Darius grinned. The two had been friends since they'd slipped through inky darkness and made their way into enemy camps in Afghanistan together. Both had been forced into retiring after sustaining injuries during their service to their country. It had been a no-brainer for Ryder to ask Darius to join the Personal Securities team, but

Darius knew him better than almost anyone, and he knew Ryder had more than a job on his mind.

Too bad.

Ryder didn't discuss his personal life on company time, and until Maureen's murderer was caught, every minute was company time.

"You can wipe the smile off your face, Darius. We both have jobs to do, and we need to keep focused on that."

"Point taken, boss." Darius bent over the computer again, but Ryder didn't miss the amusement in his voice.

He ignored it.

Shelby's door was closed and he knocked, waiting as Mazy snorted and sniffed at the bottom of the door. He shoved his foot against the crack, and the little dog barked.

"Hold on. I'm coming," Shelby called out. Seconds later, she opened the door, her eyes shadowed and dark with fatigue.

"Did I wake you?" he asked, and she shook her head, silky brown curls sliding across her cheek and down the slim column of her neck. He knew just how it would feel if he touched it, could imagine himself giving in to temptation and brushing an errant curl away.

"I never fell asleep." She lifted Mazy, held the little dog to her chest, more vulnerable and less animated than he'd ever seen her.

"Why not?" He moved into the room, catching a whiff of berries and vanilla as she backed away.

"I don't sleep well when I'm away from home." She dropped onto the bed, patting Mazy rhythmically.

"Is that the only thing that kept you awake? Being away from home?" He dropped down beside her, and she shrugged. She'd found a fitted black T-shirt and dark jeans that gapped in the back, her creamy skin peeking out between denim and cotton, her bandaged feet peeking out from brown sandals.

"Yes. No. Maybe." She offered a brief smile and placed Mazy on the floor. "I guess you didn't just knock on the door to ask if you'd woken me. What's up?"

"We're leaving for the state prison in ten minutes. I wanted to give you a heads-up."

"You only planned to give me ten minutes to get ready to go?"

"Why not? You don't need to be fancy to go visit a felon."

"Not fancy, but presentable is nice." She limped to the dresser, frowning at her reflection in the mirror above it.

"You're always way more than presentable, Shelby Ann," he responded as Mazy nipped at his ankle. "I don't think this dog likes me."

"I wish I could say the same."

"You don't want her to like you?"

"I don't want *me* to like *you*." She paced to the

window covered with a thick shade and stood with her back to Ryder.

"Because you're afraid of being disappointed again?"

"Because I have terrible taste in men, Ryder, and if I like you, there's got to be something wrong with you."

"There's plenty wrong with me. Just like there's plenty wrong with you. But that's what relationships are all about, right? Learning the good and bad about someone and accepting both."

"I don't know. I've been in too many messed-up relationships to know what a good one is."

"That doesn't mean this one has to be messed up."

"Ryder, every dream I've ever had has fallen apart, and I've gotten over it, but I don't think I could ever get over you if I started building dreams and..." Her voice trailed off, and she shrugged.

"Build all the dreams you want around me, Shelby Ann. They won't fall apart," he responded.

"How can you know that? How can I?"

"We can't if we don't try." He kneaded the tension in her shoulders, silken hair sliding over his knuckles as he leaned down, pressing a kiss to her nape.

She shivered and turned to face him, her eyes wide and wary as she met his gaze. "I think we'd better go, Ryder. If Catherine has the answers to everything that's been going on, we can't afford to miss out on an opportunity to speak with her."

She was right.

They'd better go, because they couldn't afford to miss the appointment, and because if he looked into Shelby's eyes for one more second, he might do something he wouldn't regret, but that she might.

"What time do you have to deliver the cake? The prison is an hour drive, and I want to make sure we get back in time."

"I need to be at the bakery by three. I've got to put the cake together, decorate it. I have a hundred things I need to do before I deliver it. Maybe—"

"No."

"You don't even know what I was going to say."

"You were going to ask if I could drop you off at the bakery before I went to the prison."

"I was also going to suggest that Darius come with me. That way, I'll be safe *and* productive."

"Sorry. Darius has another assignment. If he didn't, he'd be riding shotgun." He led her into the living room, grabbed a couple of protein shakes from the fridge and tossed one her way.

"Drink," he said, opening the second can and chugging the contents.

"I'd rather not."

"I'd rather not have you fainting from hunger."

She snorted but popped the lid of the can and sipped it.

"You ready to go, Darius?"

"Ready." Darius pulled a jacket over his gun holster and opened the door.

"I'll take the lead. First sign of trouble, and you take Shelby to safety."

"Will do."

"Maybe I should just stay here," Shelby said as they started down the stairs, her voice trembling slightly.

"Sorry. All my people are tied up with other assignments, and I'm not leaving you here alone." He led the way to the lobby, moving slowly, listening intently. Just because no one suspicious had showed on the monitor didn't mean they were clear. Anyone could be a threat. A friend. A neighbor. It was Ryder's job to prevent that threat from reaching Shelby.

He stepped into the lobby, scanned the area and moved to the front door.

"Stay with her, Darius. I'll get the Hummer."

He didn't wait for Darius to respond. He didn't need to. He only hired people he could count on to follow orders, people he could trust with his life, and he *could* trust Darius. Comrade in arms. Fellow SEAL. He'd give his life for a client if necessary. Ryder didn't want it to be necessary, but he knew it was true.

He surveyed the area outside the apartment, noting each person, each face, each piece of clothing. Early-morning sunlight fell across the sidewalk and gleamed on the windows of passing cars. If danger lurked nearby, Ryder didn't feel it. No hum of awareness. No hair standing on end. He got in the Hummer, driving up onto the sidewalk in front of the apartment, ignoring the shouted protests of a few disgruntled pedestrians as he opened the lobby door.

"Let's move fast." He took Shelby's arm, gesturing for Darius to fall into step beside them. Flanked on either side, Shelby seemed small, fragile and in desperate need of protection.

One bullet. That's all it would take, and she'd be lying on the pavement, her life spilling out.

He tightened his grip on her arm, adrenaline pulsing through his blood.

"Don't worry, Ryder. Everything is going to be fine," she whispered as she climbed into the Hummer, her words dancing on the cool morning air as he closed her inside.

He hoped she was right, because right at that moment they had only one lead to follow. If it didn't bring them to Shelby's attacker, they'd be at a standstill while the killer moved forward with his plans.

Catherine Miller had to be the key.

She'd been the subject of Maureen's newest project. There had to be a connection between that and Maureen's death. Ryder just had to figure out what it was.

He climbed into the Hummer, offered a quick wave in Darius's direction and pulled away.

He needed answers, and he needed them quickly, because he had a feeling the danger that was hunting Shelby was closing in. It might not have been waiting outside the apartment building, but it *was* waiting. For the right time, the right place to strike.

SIXTEEN

Catherine Miller didn't look like a cold-blooded killer.

She didn't look like the dark angel the press had portrayed her as, either.

What she looked like, Shelby thought, was a weary, wary and very tough young woman. Red hair cropped short, her face gaunt, she had a fragile build and hard blue eyes, her orange jumpsuit garish against her pale skin.

A guard led her to a chair and stood a few feet away as she settled into it.

"Thanks for seeing us today, Catherine. I'm Ryder Malone. This is Shelby Simons," Ryder began, his dark eyes completely focused on the convicted killer.

"If you're from the press, I don't do interviews," she responded, her voice softer than her eyes.

"But you allowed Maureen Lewis to interview you," Ryder said, and Catherine frowned, leaning back in the chair, blue eyes smudged with fatigue.

"I heard Maureen died. Are you family?"

"Friends," Shelby said.

"I'm sorry for your loss. Maureen was a nice lady."

"She was writing your story when she died," Ryder said, and Catherine shrugged, her shoulders narrow and way too thin. A scar snaked around her left wrist, purplish against her pale skin.

"It would be callous for me to say I wish she'd finished it before she'd died, so I won't."

"You just did," Ryder pointed out, and Catherine offered a brief smile.

"Okay. You're right. I did. I liked Maureen, but I was also excited about what she was doing. It's been four years since anyone cared to listen to my side of things. She listened, and..."

"What?" Shelby asked, imagining Maureen sitting exactly where she was, looking at the same woman, seeing someone worth trying to save.

"She believed me. Which is more than I can say for just about everyone else I know." There was a bitter edge to her voice, and Shelby wondered if she were really as innocent as she claimed or if she were just a good actress.

"What did you tell her that convinced her?" Ryder asked, and Catherine stiffened, something dark passing behind her eyes.

"You think that whatever I said got her killed, don't you?"

"Did it?"

"I don't know. I hope not, but if it did... I warned her to be careful. I told her that he..."

"What?" Ryder leaned toward her, and she shook her head.

"Look, I'm not sure why you're here, but I suggest that you go back to wherever you came from and leave Maureen to rest in peace."

"Maureen was murdered, Catherine."

"That's exactly why you need to let her rest in peace." Catherine smoothed her spiky hair, her hand shaking slightly, the hardness in her eyes only partially hiding her fear.

"If you didn't kill the patients at Good Sama—"

"I didn't."

"Then who did?"

"Like I said, you need to let Maureen rest in peace." She stood, but Ryder held up a hand.

"Give us another minute, okay?"

"Why should I? It's not like you're here to help me. You're here to help a dead woman, and she's way past that." She sat again.

"We're here because whoever murdered Maureen has been coming after Shelby. It's imperative that we find out who he is and what his motives are. You're the key to that."

"I'm sorry, but I can't help you." Catherine's gaze shifted from Ryder to Shelby, and Shelby had the feeling she really was sorry, but that there was more she knew. More she might have said.

"Can't or won't?" Ryder asked.

"Does it matter? It amounts to the same thing." She glanced back at the guard, then leaned forward, her eyes blazing with blue fire. "Be careful, okay? You seem like nice people, and I wouldn't want you to get hurt."

"Why would we?"

"For the same reason Maureen was. She asked too many questions of the wrong person and found out something she shouldn't have. Maybe she just made him nervous. Whatever the case, she's victim number twelve, and we have no reason to think he'll stop there. Don't give him reason to strike again."

"He's already tried, Catherine. Give us his name so we can stop him before he does again."

"I've already said too much."

"You haven't said anything." Ryder's irritation seeped through his words, and Shelby put a hand on his arm, his tension radiating through her palm. He covered her hand, linking their fingers.

She didn't pull away.

Didn't want to pull away.

Catherine's gazed dropped to their hands, and she offered a smile tinged with sadness. "Like I said, it's better to let Maureen rest in peace. Let the police find her killer. It's the safest thing for everyone."

Something about the way she said *everyone* made Shelby's pulse jump. Was there someone Catherine cared about? Someone she was worried about protecting? If so, that would explain her reluctance to share the information she'd given to Maureen. "Is there someone you want to send a message to, Catherine? We'd be happy to help you if we can."

Catherine hesitated, glancing at the guard again. "My grandmother. She can't drive, and I haven't seen her since I was sentenced. She's out on our old homestead outside of Spokane, still trying to work the land. She says she's doing okay, but I worry about her. I'm all the family she has, and my friends disappeared after I was convicted. Would you mind checking up on her?"

"What's her name?" Ryder said, and relief washed away the tension in Catherine's face. She looked even younger than when she'd walked in. Twenty-six or seven. Not old enough to have worked as a registered nurse, been on trial for murder, been in jail for four years.

"Eileen Miller. Maureen went to see her once and said she was doing okay. That was our deal. I'd let Maureen write my book, and she'd take care of Eileen. It's a shame things don't always work out the way they should," Catherine said as she stood.

"What's her address?"

Catherine rattled it off, ignoring the guard, who motioned that their time was up. "When you see her, tell her I love her, okay?"

"I will," Shelby said, swallowing a lump in her throat as Catherine shuffled away with the guard.

"She's not what I expected," Ryder said, taking Shelby's arm and leading her away.

"What did you expect?"

"All the articles I read about the murders made

her seem sweet and fragile. Florence Nightingale gone wrong."

"She *is* fragile."

"But she's not sweet or angelic."

"Maybe jail changed her."

"Maybe, but I don't think so. That tough edge she has came from a lifetime of hardship. Not four years of it. She seemed edgy, too. Like she wanted to say more, but was afraid. Maybe for her grandmother. Maybe for herself."

"I was thinking the same thing."

"Then I guess there's only one thing to do," he said as a guard led them back through the prison.

"What?"

"We go visit the grandmother and see what she has to say. Maybe Eileen will be more willing to talk than Catherine is, and maybe she knows what her granddaughter is hiding."

"I still need to get that wedding cake delivered," she reminded him, and he nodded.

"It's early. We should have plenty of time to stop by Eileen's place before you need to be back at the bakery."

They walked outside, bright sunlight warming the cool spring air, its heat making Shelby feel even more sluggish and tired than she already did. She had barely slept, barely eaten. Her body hurt, her head ached, and her heart....

It was going to be hurt, too.

She knew it was.

No matter what Ryder said, no matter what his intentions, eventually she'd disappoint him or he'd disappoint her. One of them would walk away and find someone else, and all the silly dreams that she kept shoving down and hiding in the deepest part of her heart would shatter.

Just like she'd told him they would.

Build as many dreams as you want around me, he'd said, and she'd been so tempted to let herself do it.

She knew better, though.

Two strikes, and she was out.

Even though she wasn't sure she wanted to be.

Ryder helped her into the Hummer, and she wondered what it would be like to be more than a client he needed to protect, more than someone he needed to keep safe. Wondered what it would be like to just let go, let herself try one more time.

"You're deep in thought, Shelby Ann," he said as he started the Hummer's engine.

"I'm just hoping that Eileen will be able to give us some helpful information, because so far, we've come up empty today."

"I wouldn't say we've come up empty. We know that Catherine is afraid *of* someone and *for* someone. We know that she thinks the same person who murdered eleven people at Good Samaritan Convalescent Center also murdered Maureen. Assuming that she's telling the truth about her innocence—"

"I think she is."

"*If* she is, coming here has proven what was only a theory before. Maureen was killed because of the research she was doing. She was killed because she got too close to a murderer who's been hiding his crimes for years."

"I agree, but we can't prove it. Not without knowing what Maureen found. Too bad all the research was destroyed in the explosion."

"Too bad for us, but not for the person who murdered Maureen."

"I hadn't thought of that." She'd just assumed that the arsonist wanted to hide his crime and make Maureen's death look like an accident, but the explosion and fire had taken all of Maureen's research with her. Everything on her computer. Everything on her cell phone.

Her entire life gone in the ring of a doorbell.

Shelby shivered, rubbing her arms to try to chase away the chill. Maureen had been so vibrantly alive, so filled with ideas and enthusiasm. Sure, she'd been demanding, but she'd also been funny and fun, caring and compassionate. She'd believed in what she did, offered nothing but full disclosure and absolute truth in her books. Evidence and facts had been everything to her, but the people behind the stories were what drove her.

She'd deserved a happier ending than what she'd gotten, and Shelby swallowed back a lump in her throat at the thought.

"Are you thinking about Maureen?" Ryder asked, and she nodded.

"How did you know?"

"Your eyes are sad."

"You're supposed to be watching the road, not me."

"I'm watching the road *and* you. You're a distraction, Shelby Ann. One I wasn't counting on when I came to Spokane."

"Where were you before?" she asked, even though she knew she shouldn't. Asking questions about his personal life was a sure way to get to know him better, and getting to know Ryder better would probably make her like him even more than she already did. In her estimation, that would be a whole lot worse than falling for him. If she fell, she could right herself. If she liked him more and more, she couldn't turn away.

"New York City. That's where I keep the main office of my business."

"You have more than one office?"

"This is my fourth. I already had offices in New York, Florida and Texas. A friend of mine suggested I open one here, and it seemed like a good idea. Mid-Atlantic, southeast and southwest. Now, the northwest. I came here four months ago, so I could spend a year setting things up."

"And create a security monopoly?" she responded, his words leaving her hollow.

He'd been in town four months.

Was going home in eight.

Build all the dreams you want around me.

But that would be difficult to do if he wasn't around.

"Not quite."

"The sheriff said your business is one of the best in the country."

"That's a matter of opinion, and I've never been overly concerned about people's opinions."

"Then what are you concerned with?"

"Keeping you safe."

"Aside from that."

"If I didn't know better, I'd think you were curious about me." He shot a glance in her direction, his eyes filled with amusement.

"We've been spending a lot of time together. It's only natural to be curious."

"Yeah?"

"Yes," she said firmly, and he chuckled.

"So, what else do you want to know?"

"Nothing."

"Liar."

"Everything, then, but that would be dangerous, wouldn't it, Ryder? Because in a few months you'll go back to New York, and I'll be here, working in my bakery, wishing I hadn't spent so much time getting to know you."

"Just because I *planned* to stick around for a year doesn't mean I'll *only* stick around for a year," he responded.

"It doesn't mean you'll stick around longer, either."

"I guess how long I stay will depend on what I'll be leaving behind." His words hung in the air, and Shelby knew he was waiting for her to respond, waiting for her to stop being a coward and start going after what she wanted.

The problem was, what she *didn't* want kept getting in her way.

Three strikes.

And the last one would be too painful to ever recover from.

Ryder pulled onto the interstate, accelerating into sparse traffic and putting distance between them and Catherine Miller.

A woman behind bars for a crime she said she hadn't committed, stuck there because she had no power to free herself.

Sometimes, Shelby felt the same way.

Powerless to free herself from past mistakes, from self-doubt, from fear.

Powerless despite all the power she had.

Faith. Family. Friends.

She didn't live behind bars. Her prison was one of her own making, but it was no less real, and Shelby was unable to break free, no matter how much she wanted to.

Tell her I love her.

That's all Catherine had asked, but Shelby thought she wanted more. Wanted something so desperately she hadn't dared mention it.

Freedom to leave the prison, to reach out for all the things she didn't dare dream she'd ever have.

In that small way, at least, they were exactly the same.

SEVENTEEN

Ryder's cell phone rang as he pulled up in front of a faded clapboard farmhouse. He grabbed it, glancing at Shelby as he answered. She'd fallen asleep, her head resting against the window, her hair falling across her cheek. If he'd had the time, he would have driven around for a while longer, let her get the sleep she obviously needed, but he didn't.

Not just because Shelby had a wedding cake to decorate and deliver, but because danger was breathing down their necks. They couldn't afford to do anything but keep pushing hard for the answers that would lead them to the killer. Finding him was the only way to stop him, the only way to keep Shelby safe.

"Ryder Malone." He kept his voice low, hoping she'd get at least a few extra minutes of rest.

"This is Deputy Sheriff Logan Randal."

"What can I do for you, Randal?"

"Put Shelby Simons on the phone. She *is* with you, right?"

"Yes, the sheriff and I agreed she'd be safer that way."

"May I speak to her?"

"She's not available."

"Yes, I am," Shelby mumbled as she lifted her head and opened her eyes. They were red-rimmed and deeply shadowed, her skin so pale it was almost translucent.

"I thought you were asleep."

"Just resting my eyes. Is it Dottie?"

"Deputy Sheriff Randal," he said, handing her the phone. He wanted to smooth the frown line from her forehead, but she'd been on edge since they'd left the state prison, and he figured it had more to do with him than it had to do with meeting Catherine.

Afraid, that's what she was.

So afraid that she wouldn't allow herself to accept what she felt, believe it could last.

"Hello?" She pressed the phone to her ear, her eyes wide and wary as she watched him. She listened for a moment. "Monday? I think that will work."

"What will work?" Ryder asked, and Shelby slapped her palm over his mouth.

"I'm trying to hear," she whispered, her palm so smooth and silky he didn't see any reason to push it away. "Okay. I'll see you then, Deputy Randal." Her hand dropped away, and she handed Ryder the phone.

"Well?"

"They rescheduled the sketch artist because of the fire. She'll be here Monday. The sheriff is going to send a patrol car to bring me to the station once she arrives."

"I'll bring you."

"There's no need. Not if I have a police escort."

"There's every need." He got out of the Hummer and opened Shelby's door. He'd be bringing her to the sheriff's office whether she liked it or not, and no amount of arguing would change that, but she didn't seem intent on arguing.

Her gaze was focused on the old house and its overgrown yard. A storm door hung on broken hinges, the screen gutted out. Brown grass surrounded the dilapidated building, but beyond it, the land looked lush and green. The fields, at least, were being tended.

"The place looks abandoned. Do you think we're at the right house?"

"We're at the right address. Unless something happened to Catherine's grandmother, she must still be living here."

"Maybe, but she's not living very well. Look, two of the windows are broken. The roof has a hole in it. What does she do in the winter? What does she do when it rains?"

"Good question. How about we knock on the door and ask?"

"You, there! Get out of here!" a voice called from an open window on the first floor as Ryder opened the gate. The faded blue curtain rustled, but there was no sign of the speaker.

She was there, though, hidden behind the fabric.

Ryder focused his attention there and called out. "We're here to see Eileen. Is she around?"

"I said, get out of here."

"Catherine sent us to make sure her grandmother was doing all right. We're not leaving until we do that." Shelby stepped forward, and Ryder tugged her back. For all he knew, the speaker had a gun aimed at one of their heads.

He touched his weapon, the Glock warm and smooth beneath his fingers.

"Are you Catherine's friends?" The curtains pulled back, and a red-haired woman looked out, her face tan and deeply wrinkled, her cheeks hollow. She looked gaunt and jaundiced, cigarette smoke floating through the window and out into the yard.

"We met with her, hoping to get information about a case we're working on. She mentioned her grandmother, and we offered to check in and see how Eileen is doing. Is she here?"

"She's here, and she's glad you didn't say you were Catherine's friends. My granddaughter doesn't have any that visit her or me. Not anymore. Hold on a minute. I'll let you in."

A few minutes passed before the door swung open, the rusted hinges squeaking as Eileen motioned them inside. She wore faded jeans and a bright pink tank top, both her arms covered in faded tattoos, a cigarette held between her fingers. Nothing like the frail grandmother Ryder had expected, but her hand shook as she waved them toward the living room, and he understood why Catherine had worried so much about her welfare.

"Come on in. I don't have all day."

"You're Eileen?" Ryder asked, and the woman nodded, closing the door and turning the lock and bolt.

"Who else would I be? Who else would live in a dump like this? Go ahead and sit. Might as well get comfortable." She lowered herself into a worn easy chair, wincing with the movement. "So, what do you want?"

"Catherine is worried about you. She wanted us to make sure you were okay," Shelby responded, gingerly sitting on the edge of a sagging sofa.

Ryder stood, afraid to test the strength of any of the rickety furniture.

"That's not the only reason you're here, is it? It's not like you know my granddaughter, and it's not like you care about her or about me. So, what do you really want?" She stubbed the cigarette out in an overflowing ashtray, her thick-veined hand trembling violently.

Fear?

Illness?

A combination of both?

Ryder wasn't sure, and he studied her as she

studied Shelby. Eyebrows drawn on. No eyelashes. Lips pale.

Cancer?

He hoped not.

For her sake and for Catherine's.

"We're here for exactly the reason I said. To make sure you're okay," Shelby responded to her question, and Eileen's scowl deepened.

"Don't lie to me, girl. I don't like it."

"Why would I lie?" Shelby stood her ground.

"Because lying is what people do. Even highbrow, fancy ladies like you."

"I'm not highbrow or—"

"Eileen, we also want to find out what you know about Maureen Lewis's death," Ryder cut in, and Eileen turned her attention to him.

"The true-crime writer, right? Got blown up in her house. Police determined that she was murdered."

"That's right."

"I heard about it on the news." Eileen pulled out another cigarette, tapped it against her knee.

"She was writing a book about the murders that your granddaughter committed."

"She was convicted, but she wasn't guilty," Eileen snapped.

"That's not what a jury of her peers thought."

"Catherine was railroaded by the system."

"Do you know how many family members of

convicts think that?" Ryder didn't pull his punches, and Shelby grabbed his arm, shook her head.

He ignored her.

Whatever information Eileen had, they needed it.

"Plenty, but I'm not one of them. I know my granddaughter, and I know the things she's capable of. Murder isn't one of them."

"Someone killed those patients, Eileen," Shelby said quietly, and Eileen nodded.

"Exactly, and that's how Catherine got herself into trouble. She reported the murders. Did you know that?"

"No." Ryder knew very little about the case except what he'd read in old newspaper articles.

"It's true. There were several patients at Good Samaritan that Catherine was really close to. She met them when she was still a nurse's aide, and she continued to care for them after she became an RN. None of them had any family close by, so she'd bring them little trinkets and go to visit them when she was off duty. That's the kind of girl Catherine is."

"But?" Ryder pressed her to continue and she frowned, staring up at the ceiling as if she could find answers there.

"Flu season rolled around and four of those patients died in less than three months. Complications from the flu. That's what the families were told, but Catherine knew that none of them had been sick. She started keeping track after that. Two more patients died in the next five months. Neither of them were sick, either. Being the kind of girl she is, Catherine took the information to the local police, and they started to investigate. Next thing we knew, Catherine was being accused of murder." She lit the cigarette, took a long drag and blew a stream of smoke into the air.

"Accused based on what evidence?" Ryder asked, and Eileen shrugged.

"Three of the patients who died left my granddaughter money. One of them left her entire estate to Catherine. Really ticked off the woman's granddaughter. She requested an autopsy. The results were inconclusive, but the woman still insisted that Catherine had manipulated her grandmother into changing her will. She planted the seed of suspicion. The police watered it. They hunted for months until they found evidence to arrest Catherine. Evidence someone else planted."

"You're saying someone murdered eleven people and then framed your granddaughter?"

"That's exactly what I'm saying. Who knows whether he was trying to pin it on her from the beginning or if she offered herself up by going to the police? All I know is that it worked. She's in jail. The real murderer is free."

"Circumstantial evidence doesn't get a person convicted, Eileen," Ryder said.

"If you'd done your homework, you'd already know what got her convicted."

"I haven't had a whole lot of time for homework, so why don't you fill me in?"

"The police found a syringe with traces of potassium chloride in Catherine's purse. Her fingerprints were on it. They also found a bottle of potassium chloride in her work locker, and one under the seat in her car. It was all over the news, and she was pretty much publicly convicted before she ever went to trial," Shelby offered quietly, her eyes filled with compassion.

"What's your name, girl?" Eileen responded.

"Shelby Simons."

"Well, Shelby, here's the rest of what you need to know. Part of my granddaughter's job was to administer medications. Sometimes orally. Sometimes through injections. She touched dozens of syringes a day. Anyone could have taken a syringe she'd used, filled it with potassium and emptied it out again. Anyone could have stuck a bottle of poison in her locker or put one in her car. She never bothered to lock either. Besides, Catherine is one smart cookie. She graduated from high school two years early and had her nursing degree by the time she was twenty. No way would she be stupid enough to leave the evidence around if she *was* a murderer. Which she isn't."

"If she didn't murder her patients, who did?" Ryder asked, and Eileen shrugged.

"That's the question, isn't it? Catherine thought she knew, and she told anyone who would listen, but it didn't do her any good. The prosecutors had their scapegoat, and they knew they'd get an easy conviction. A poor girl from the wrong side of the tracks, no one but an old grandmother and a couple of troublemaking friends to help her. Catherine didn't stand a chance." Eileen took another drag of the cigarette, coughing as she blew the smoke out.

"Who did *she* think the murderer was?" Ryder's nerves hummed with excitement, blood racing through his veins in quick, hard bursts. All they needed was a name. Once they had that, they'd know what direction to go, which way to look.

"She told me not to say."

"Why?"

"Because she was worried about me. That girl's heart is too soft. She said she'd spend the rest of her life in jail if it meant keeping me safe. Like I'm going to live the rest of *her* life. Don't know where that child gets her heart from. It doesn't come from my side of the family, that's for sure."

"Did you give Maureen the person's name?"

"Of course I did. No way would I let my granddaughter rot in prison. Next thing I knew, Maureen was dead. Catherine was still in prison."

"Who did Catherine suspect?"

"A doctor. Guy named Christopher Peterson. Nice upright member of the community. A guy no one would ever suspect."

"But Catherine did?" Adrenaline shot through Ryder. Finally, a name.

"He had access to the patients who died. He was at Good Samaritan on the days of their deaths. He was arrogant enough to think he knew what was best for everyone who walked through the doors, and he wasn't as upright as he wanted everyone to believe. He had asked Catherine out a few times after she started working there. Seeing as how he was married and had three kids, it wasn't something she was interested in."

"The fact that he was a player isn't a reason to suspect him of murder," Ryder said. But it was something to go on. Which was a lot more than they'd had an hour ago.

"Didn't you hear a word I said, boy? Aside from Catherine, he was the only one working at Good Samaritan every day that a patient died. The defense brought him up as another possible suspect, but there was nothing to link him to the potassium, and he'd been called home on emergencies before two of the patients died."

"So, he had an alibi." Shelby sounded disappointed, but an alibi didn't mean a person was innocent. It just meant he was good at covering his crimes.

"Doesn't mean he didn't do it." Eileen took another drag on her cigarette, frowning as she exhaled. "I promised Catherine I'd quit these cancer sticks, but so far I've only been able to cut back."

"Bad habits are hard to break," Ryder responded by rote, his thoughts on the information Eileen had provided. Another suspect. A man whom the community trusted, whom his patients trusted. Was it possible *he* was the real murderer?

"You're telling me. So—" she stubbed out the second cigarette "—is there anything else you need?"

"No, but before we go, Eileen, Catherine had a message she wanted us to give you," Shelby said as Eileen struggled to her feet.

"What's that?"

"She said to tell you that she loves you."

"Yeah?" Eileen blinked rapidly, her eyes moist and bright. "That girl. Her heart is too soft. That's been the problem all along."

"If you'd like, I can take you to visit her next week," Shelby offered, and Eileen's expression brightened.

"Anytime. Just give me a call. My number is listed. I can pay you for gas, but that's about it. Funds have been short since Catherine went to prison."

"I wouldn't want payment, Ms. Eileen." Shelby kept talking as Ryder tried to hurry her out of the living room and back to the Hummer. Catherine wasn't the only one with a soft heart. Shelby had one, too. In his mind, that only made her more vulnerable.

He wanted to tell her to guard that part of herself, but Shelby's softness intrigued him as much as her silky hair and sweet smile. More than either of those things, because it stemmed from something deep in her soul.

All Ryder had to do was look in her eyes, and he saw it. All he had to do was listen to her with her employees and with Dottie, and he heard it.

She was soft, and he was soft for her, and there was nothing he could do to change either of those things.

Nothing he *would* do to change it.

"I'll call you next week," Shelby said, and Eileen nodded.

"I'll be around. Now, you two go on back to what you were doing, and watch out. It seems to me that Maureen would have been a lot better off if she'd stayed out of things that weren't her business."

"It was her business. She was writing your granddaughter's story, remember?" Ryder said as they walked to the door.

"Not Catherine's story. That scum Peterson's story. A poor choice. Better make sure you're not making any, or you might wind up the same way she did. You both seem like nice kids. I wouldn't want to see you hurt."

Shelby stiffened at her words, her muscles tightening beneath Ryder's hand. "We'll be careful."

They stepped outside, the wooden floorboards of the porch giving a little under Ryder's weight. Obviously, Eileen was falling behind on the upkeep of her property. The clapboard house was faded, its paint peeling and gray. Maybe it had been beautiful a long time ago. Now it simply looked tired, the overgrown yard edging in and threatening to overtake the house and rickety porch. He'd send some of his men over to straighten things out. A little overtime wouldn't hurt any of them.

"That was…interesting," Shelby said as she climbed into the Hummer, her borrowed jeans hugging curvy hips and long, lean legs.

He tried not to notice, but that was difficult when the breeze carried hints of berries and vanilla. Difficult when every moment of every day seemed to be filled with Shelby.

Every thought.

Every decision based on what would keep her safe.

"I'd say it was informative. I think that a meeting with Dr. Peterson will be even more so," he responded, shutting the door and shutting down his errant thoughts.

"That means we're not going to the bakery yet, doesn't it?" She brushed stray curls from her cheek, watching him as he got into the Hummer and started the engine. He shouldn't feel her gaze the way he felt the sunlight pouring in the window, but he did.

"Sorry, but we need to visit Dr. Peterson. I want to get his take on things. We should still have plenty of time for that cake you need to build."

"Stack. Not build. And I have to put flowers on it, too."

"I'll help you."

"You can help me by getting me back to the bakery by three."

"I'll give it my best shot."

"Do you really think the doctor will be willing to talk to us?"

"We won't know until we ask." He grabbed his cell phone and dialed the office, waiting impatiently while it rang.

"Personal Securities, Inc—"

"It's Ryder," he cut in, and Paisley Duncan huffed.

"You could have waited until I finished, boss," she said, and he knew she was fidgeting at the desk, wishing she were out doing something more exciting. That had been her M.O. since he'd hired the twentysomething office temp. She wanted to be a bodyguard. Not office help.

Too bad she didn't have any training.

Too bad she couldn't fire a gun.

Too bad there was no way *ever* that Ryder would assign her a case.

"I have more important things on my mind than manners, Paisley. I need you to track down a doctor named Christopher Peterson. He works at Good Samaritan in—"

"The valley. Right. I know it. My grandmother was there for a couple of years."

"Call them and see if Peterson is in today. If he is there, let me know. If he's not, ask when he'll be in next."

"You want me to set up an appointment for you to meet with him?"

"I'd prefer he not know I'm coming. I don't want him taking off to avoid a meeting."

"I can find his home address, too. We could—"

"*We're* not doing anything."

"You take all the fun out of this job, you know that, boss?"

"Call Good Samaritan. Let me know what you find out. I should be hitting town in an hour. I need the information before then." He disconnected before Paisley could beg him to bring her to the interview. Fresh out of college with a master's degree in English, she had no business doing anything but writing the next great American novel she was working on and sitting at a desk, and that's exactly what he'd told her on too many occasions to count.

"We're not just going to show up at the convalescent center without warning and confront the doctor, are we?" Shelby sounded appalled.

"We're going to show up there, his home, the hospital. Wherever he is, because I need to talk to him, and letting him know I'm coming will only give him time to compose his thoughts."

"I have a wedding cake to prep and deliver, Ryder. I can't spend the afternoon chasing down a doctor. If he's not at Good Samaritan—"

"Then we're going to have to keep looking. Your life is more important than a wedding cake."

"Maybe not to the bride," she grumbled, and he patted her knee, his hand resting on worn denim.

She stilled, her muscles taut, and he was sure she was holding her breath, waiting for him to move away.

Or to claim more than a pat on the knee.

Velvety lips, whispered sighs, sweet smiles.

He wanted more of them all when the time was right, but it wasn't right. Not yet.

"We'll be back at the bakery in plenty of time for you to do what needs to be done." He lifted his hand, ignoring the warmth that thrummed through his veins.

"I'm already behind, so there's no way I'll have plenty of time."

"Two hands will cut the time by half."

"Or double it. You don't know your way around a wedding cake any more than I do the revolver you're carrying."

"It's a semiautomatic, Shelby Ann, and I can teach you anything you want to know about it the same way you can teach me about wedding cakes."

"But—"

His cell phone rang, and he grabbed it, knowing exactly who it was before he answered. Paisley was overly eager, but she was also smart and quick.

"Ryder, here."

"I have the information you want, boss. Peterson is stopping in at the convalescent center today. He's scheduled to be there from noon to three."

"Then we're in business. Thanks, Paisley."

"Thank me by taking me wi—"

He disconnected, cutting her off before she could ask. He'd trained people to work as security contractors, but he didn't plan to train her. She was too eager and too young, and that could get her or a client killed.

"He's there?" Shelby asked, and he nodded.

"He'll be there until three." Which worked out perfectly. They'd find him while he was working his shift and ask a few questions before he knew why they were there. Hopefully they would throw him off balance and prevent him from formulating polished, practiced replies.

Ryder would know if the doctor was lying. Gaze shifting, hands fidgeting, stance tense, subtle clues that would give him away, and Ryder would be watching for them.

Maybe the doctor wouldn't lie, though.

Maybe he'd tell the truth.

Maybe, but Ryder thought another possibility was more likely.

The doctor *would* lie, and he'd keep on lying.

Because, Ryder thought, Dr. Christopher Peterson probably had a very good reason for doing so.

EIGHTEEN

Christopher Peterson didn't look any more like a cold-blooded killer than Catherine had. The thought flitted through Shelby's mind as she followed Ryder and the doctor into a small office.

Peterson didn't look like a killer, but he didn't look happy, either. As a matter of fact, he'd been looking decidedly *un*happy since Ryder had introduced himself and Shelby and asked if they could speak to him.

"I appreciate you giving us a few minutes of your time, Dr. Peterson," Ryder said as the doctor closed the office door.

"You should, because I don't have a few minutes. As a matter of fact, I don't have any time at all."

"Then that makes us even more appreciative," Ryder responded, but there was little sincerity in his words. He looked predatory and fierce, focused and dangerous, his attention never wavering from the doctor's face.

"Right. Whatever you want to ask, ask quickly."

Dr. Peterson dropped into a leather armchair, his receding hair standing up around a broad, slightly jowly face, his emerald eyes flashing with irritation.

"We were hoping you could tell us a little bit about the murders that were committed here." Ryder didn't beat around the bush, and the doctor tensed, his eyes narrowing.

"That's old news, and you can find whatever information you need by requesting the case file from the police or visiting the library and looking at back issues of the local newspaper. Every horrible detail is there." He rubbed the bridge of his nose, age spots marring the too-smooth skin on the back of his hand.

"I'm not interested in what the police or the newspaper have to say, Doctor. I'm interested in what *you* have to say. The way I've heard it, Catherine Miller wasn't the only employee who worked every shift that a patient died on. You were working those shifts, too."

"The police knew that. The prosecutor knew it, but none of them cared, because they already had their murderer. Like I said, it's all old news."

"You were called away from the hospital during three of the shifts, right? When you returned, you found the deceased."

"It's been a long time, but that sounds about right."

"I wouldn't think any amount of time could make it difficult to remember. Eleven people died."

"Did you come here to accuse me of something,

Mr. Malone?" The doctor leaned forward, his eyes narrow with anger.

"I just wanted your take on things. Catherine Miller is still insisting she's innocent. Maybe she's telling the truth. What do you think?"

"I think she's crazy. I thought it the first day we met, and I thought it every day I worked with her."

"Even the day you asked her out?" Ryder asked, and the doctor stood.

"I think this conversation is over."

"You did ask her out, right?"

"What does that have to do with the death of eleven innocent people?"

"I'm just trying to get the facts straight."

"The facts are that Catherine Miller injected potassium chloride into eleven patients over the course of her two years here. They died, and she went to prison for her crimes. Justice was served, and we've all moved on."

"Not everyone is convinced Catherine is a murderer."

"I'm convinced. People who work here are convinced. The families of her victims are convinced. What the rest of the world thinks doesn't really matter." The doctor paced to a small window that looked out over the parking area, his back ramrod straight.

"Do you know Maureen Lewis?" Ryder asked,

and Dr. Peterson swung around, his eyes cold and hard.

"She's the woman that died in a house fire a few days ago, right? The true-crime writer?"

"She was investigating the Good Samaritan murders for a book she was working on. We thought maybe she'd interviewed you."

"She was here. We only had a minute to talk, though. A few days later, she was dead. A shame. It's one thing for a person to live a full life and then go peacefully, knowing they've lived long and happily, and that they won't be burdens to their families any longer. It's another thing for someone to die young." The doctor's hot, angry gaze settled on Shelby, and her skin crawled. She resisted the urge to step behind Ryder, meeting Peterson's eyes head-on.

"You think the fact that someone is elderly means he's a burden?" she asked, and Peterson frowned.

"Not at all. I'm simply saying that death is inevitable, but it's much easier to accept when the person who dies has lived a long and fulfilling life. Now, if you'll excuse me, I have some patients to see." He walked out of the room without a backward glance.

"He's not very warm and fuzzy. I wonder what his bedside manner is like," Shelby said as Ryder led her out of the office.

"I'm thinking that I'd rather not find out."

"For someone who works at a convalescent facility, he didn't seem all that compassionate toward the elderly."

"I was thinking the same thing. As a matter of fact, I can't think of any reason why a guy like that would be committed to keeping the infirm or dying alive, and I can't help wondering why he's working here."

"Because it pays the bills?"

"Or because he gets a kick out of playing God," Ryder said quietly as they walked through the corridor, his words just loud enough for Shelby to hear.

"Do you really think he's a murderer?" she whispered back, and Ryder shrugged.

"He had the means, and I'm not sure how good his alibi was. The patients aren't hooked to monitors here like they are at the hospital. Peterson could have administered the poison and left the hospital before the deaths were discovered."

"I'm sure the police thought of that."

"I'm sure they did, too, but remember what Peterson said? They knew a lot of things, but it didn't matter because they already had their suspect. One who had the murder weapon hidden in her car, her locker and her purse. It would be interesting to know if the police were as thorough in their investigation of Peterson as they were of Catherine once they found those vials. When we get to the bakery, I'm going to call the sheriff and see what he has to say."

"So, we're finally going to the bakery?" Shelby's

heart jumped with anticipation, the anxiety that had been gnawing at her for the better part of the day easing slightly. It was late, but she still had time to put the cake together and deliver it.

If she hurried, and she would, because people were counting on her and she couldn't bear to let them down.

"I told you I'd bring you there when we finished here."

"You told me you'd bring me there after we finished at the prison, then after we finished at Eileen's, then—"

"I get it, Shelby Ann. You're disappointed that I didn't follow through on what I said, but I'll make it up to you."

Disappointed wasn't at all how she felt.

Scared.

Anxious.

Worried.

Those topped her list.

Compelled and intrigued rounded out the end of it.

Or maybe they were the beginning.

When Ryder was around, she didn't know up or down or sideways. She only knew that being with him felt better than being with any other man she'd ever known.

That couldn't be a good thing, but it felt as if it was.

Ryder got in the Hummer, his dark eyes skimming over her, and her heart beat hard for him, her pulse racing.

She turned away.

She didn't want to look into his eyes, not wanting to see her longings reflected in his face.

Shelby had always believed that if she worked hard, prayed hard and tried hard, she'd get the things she wanted in life. Now, she was on the cusp of her thirtieth birthday, and she had a murderer chasing after her and a too-handsome bodyguard that was bound to break her heart if she let him. She had a dog she'd inherited from a friend who should have lived way longer than fifty years and a pile of ash instead of a house.

But she also had Dottie and Zane and Rae. She had her mother and sister and her friends. She had her bakery. She had her faith.

And maybe, just maybe, she had Ryder, too.

For now.

But not forever.

As long as she remembered that, she'd be just fine.

She rubbed the itchy, achy area surrounding the stitches in her back, remembering the firm, hot touch of his hands as he'd massaged the spasms out of her muscles.

For now.

Not forever.

She really *did* need to remember that.

Which was why she needed to forget his touch,

his kisses, his gentleness, and she needed to concentrate on what had to be done to get the wedding cake ready for delivery.

She grabbed the door handle as Ryder pulled up in front of Just Desserts, ready to hop out of the Hummer and run into the building, but he grabbed her shoulder, pulling her back.

"Wait until I come around."

"The door is—"

"Wait," he growled, and she decided to do what he asked rather than waste more time arguing. Finish the cake. Deliver it. Then she could retreat to the safe house, lock herself in her room there and pretend her life hadn't completely fallen apart.

Several customers stared out the bakery's front window as Ryder rounded the Hummer, his jacket swinging open to reveal his side holster and gun. He looked tough, handsome and a little terrifying, and more than one woman leaned close to the glass, ogling him as he opened the door and ushered Shelby out of the vehicle.

She couldn't blame them.

She'd be ogling, too, if she weren't so busy running beside him as he hurried her into the bakery.

Conversation ceased as they entered the building, three dozen pairs of eyes following them as they walked around the glass display case and into the service area where Dottie worked shoulder to shoulder with Rae and Zane.

"It's about time you two showed up. We've been

swamped since we opened. People coming in and asking me a million questions about you and your house. Asking me if you were alive or dead. The nerve! That's what I told them, too. The nerve!" Dottie said as she handed a white box to a customer.

"Sorry. Things took longer than we expected." Shelby grabbed an apron from a hook near the register and put it on. The cake still needed work, but she couldn't leave Dottie and Rae with lines ten customers long. Besides, running into the back and hiding from the gawking patrons wouldn't change what had happened. It certainly wouldn't fix her house.

"It's been fine, Shelby. Dottie is just grumpy because she's been worrying about you. She made me drive her by your place to see how bad the damage was, and she nearly had a heart attack," Zane said as he filled a box with frosted-yellow chocolate cupcakes.

"The house can be replaced," Shelby responded, and Dottie frowned.

"But *you* can't. You could have died in that fire, just like poor Maureen. And you!" She pointed a gnarled finger at Ryder. "You're fired. I'm shipping my girl off to Europe for a month, so you're not needed anymore. Maybe by the time she gets back the police will have caught the guy who's trying to kill her." Dottie rang up another customer, shoving a half-dozen chocolate-chip cookies into a box and passing it to the wide-eyed, gap-jawed young woman who'd just paid.

"I can't go to Europe. I have a business to run and a cake to deliver to a wedding tonight." Shelby grabbed a dozen apple Danishes from the display case and packaged them for a regular customer.

"Forget the wedding and the business, doll. I promised your grandmother that I'd look out for you if she died before I did, and that's what I'm doing. I have money socked away. Enough to send you first-class to Paris. Maybe you'll meet some gorgeous French guy, and—"

"You'll have to buy two tickets, Dottie. Once you hire me, I can't be fired," Ryder responded as Shelby rang up the customer.

"Maybe if you were doing a better job, I wouldn't have to fire you," Dottie griped, and the customer offered Shelby a sympathetic smile before walking away.

Shelby filled another order as Dottie and Ryder discussed plans for her life, and she didn't say a word. What good would it do? Both were as stubborn and hardheaded as mules. Besides, she didn't know what she could add to the conversation. She had no idea how to keep herself safe or how to end the nightmare she'd somehow found herself in.

She rang up another order and then left the service area. Silent and comforting, the kitchen offered the solace she needed. She grabbed the sugar flowers and rolled the chilled cakes out of the fridge, frosting and assembling the first two layers quickly. One large round, then another smaller round. She piped abstract swirls on the buttercream, using a pastry bag and white decorator icing that added depth and dimension to the cake.

"It's beautiful." Ryder's words cut through the silence, and Shelby screamed, whirling around, icing squirting from the end of the piping bag onto the front of her apron.

"You did it again! I told you not to keep sneaking up on me."

"Sorry about that. You okay?" He took the piping bag and wiped icing from her apron, his hand swiping her abdomen, spreading heat with every touch.

She stepped back and bumped the counter, her cheeks heating as Ryder smiled.

He knew exactly what his touch did to her.

"I'm busy. There's a lot to do before we can transport this cake." She turned back to her work, the skin on the back of her neck burning as his gaze swept over her.

"How can I help?"

"Go back up front and help in the service area." She finished the last piped swirl and lifted a flower, gently pushing the stem through buttercream and cake.

"Not a possibility. Dottie threatened me with bodily injury if I got within ten feet of her." He lifted a delicate lily of the valley and held it out to her, his long, tan fingers gentle on the gumpaste bloom.

"I can't believe a guy like you would be afraid of a woman like Dottie."

"I'm not afraid of her. I'm afraid of what it will mean for us if she decides she doesn't like me. I know how close the two of you are." He handed her another flower, and Shelby placed it on the top tier, not daring to meet Ryder's eyes.

"There is no us."

"If you say so, Shelby Ann." He took a flower from the tray, placed it next to the one she'd already affixed to the cake.

"I do." But she wasn't sure she meant it.

"Why? Because of a couple of failed attempts at love with a couple of guys who didn't deserve you? Are you really going to let them steal your possibilities?" He stepped closer, looking down into her eyes as if he could read the truth there.

"I'm not letting them steal anything. Now, if you don't mind, I really do have to work. Since you can't go up front without facing the wrath of Dottie, how about you sit in my office while I finish this? We need to leave here in less than an hour."

"Your office is a closet, and I think I'd rather watch you work."

"I'd rather you not," she muttered as she placed another flower on the cake.

You're not going to let them steal your possibilities.

His words spun through her mind as she placed another flower and another.

She didn't have time to dwell on his assessment of her life. She needed to completely cover the top tier of the cake with sugar blossoms before she transported it. That had to be her one and only focus, but the next flower she lifted broke, her grip too tight, her concentration shot.

"Better be careful, Shelby. We're not going to have time to make replacement flowers," he said.

"It wouldn't have broken if you weren't standing there staring at me."

"Watching. There's a big difference between that and staring."

"Watching. Staring. Who cares? All I know is that you're making me nervous." The words slipped out, and her cheeks heated again.

"There are lots of things you should be nervous about. I'm not one of them."

"That's a matter of opinion." She placed another flower, filling in the last of the top tier and carefully placing it in a box. One more tier, and she'd be ready to go. Out of the kitchen, out in the fresh air where she could breathe without catching a whiff of Ryder's masculine scent.

She began piping the third layer, squirted a line too thick and had to scrape it off and begin again.

"Want some help?" Ryder asked, a hint of amusement in his voice.

"It's not funny, Ryder."

"I'm not laughing." He took the piping bag from her hands and set it on the counter, smoothing his palms up her arms until they cupped her biceps.

"I have to finish," she protested, but she didn't reach for the bag, couldn't stop looking into his dark eyes.

"You have time."

"Not for this."

"There's always time for this," he murmured, leaning down so they were a breath apart. "Because there's something you don't seem to understand and that I need to explain. You are everything a man could want. Soft and sweet and strong and brave. The two failures you keep telling me about. They weren't yours, and when we finally have time for us, there isn't going to be another one."

"Ryder—" Her breath caught as he touched the corner of her mouth, traced a line from there to the hollow of her throat.

"Are you still nervous? Or is something else making your heart beat so fast?"

"Both."

"I hope that that something else is me." His lips brushed hers, light, easy. She sighed because she couldn't do anything else. Not protest. Not pull back. Not think of one reason why she shouldn't enjoy the moment.

He tugged her closer, and she went willingly, her arms sliding around his waist as he deepened the kiss, carried her away from the shop and the cake and all the worries that had been weighing her down.

"You're supposed to be her bodyguard, Malone. Not her hunk of burnin' love." Dottie's voice was like a splash of ice water in the face, and Shelby jumped back.

"Don't you have customers to help, Dottie?" Ryder asked, his tone gruff and raw.

That would have made Shelby feel better about her heaving breaths if Dottie hadn't been glowering at her.

"We cleared the crowd, and I thought I'd give Shelby a hand getting this cake out the door, but apparently she's less worried about that than I thought."

"I'm almost finished." Shelby lifted the piping bag and added a loose swirl to the side of the tier, her hand shaking so much she almost made another blob instead.

"You would have been finished if you'd kept your mind on the job." Dottie motioned for Ryder to grab the two layers Shelby had already assembled. "Let's get these out to the car while she finishes the last tier. You know this wedding is at a park, right?"

"It was on the schedule. Manito Park. The Japanese gardens, and I've already got my men doing a sweep of the area."

"Humph." Dottie seemed less than impressed by Ryder's preparedness. "Let's move, then. Time is ticking away, and the wedding reception isn't going to wait for you to arrive."

"We still have time, Dottie," Shelby said, but Dottie was too busy bustling Ryder from the room to hear her.

Shelby finished the tier quickly, her hand steadier as she piped swirls, placed flowers and boxed it up.

Done.

And she'd still be leaving on time.

Despite the kiss.

She lifted the cake box, balancing it carefully as she grabbed extra icing, and started to walk out of the kitchen.

"Wait." Ryder grabbed her arm as he walked back in, pulling her to a stop, his phone pressed to his ear.

"No. Sorry. Go ahead." He listened silently to the speaker, his gaze never leaving Shelby. "Good. I'm glad to hear that. Thanks, Sheriff." He hung up, took the box from her hand.

"Ready to go?"

"Yes. What did the sheriff say?"

"Mostly what we've already heard. The police investigated Peterson after Catharine contacted them, but the evidence against her was compelling and Peterson had an alibi for at least two of the murders. That took him off the suspect list. His name came up during the investigation into Maureen's murder, though, and he admitted to meeting with her twice."

"So, he's a suspect again?"

"He's a person of interest, but there's really no

evidence that he had anything to do with Maureen's murder. He was home the entire night before the explosion. His wife is willing to testify to that."

"He wasn't the man I saw that morning. I'm sure of that, and if that guy is the one coming after me, I don't think we can accuse Peterson of murdering Maureen."

"It's not as difficult as you might think to hire someone to do your dirty work. You can buy almost anything for the right price. Even someone's death."

"But Peterson wouldn't have any reason to want me dead, Ryder. I have nothing that would lead the police to him. I'd never even met him before today."

"That doesn't mean he's not connected to the attacks. If he hired someone to murder Maureen, and if you saw that person on your way to Maureen's house, he might want to make sure you can't point the finger at him."

"So, Peterson doesn't want me dead, the assassin he hired does?"

"It's possible. We won't know for sure until we find the guy. Wait here. I'm going to put this in the Hummer, and then I'm going to escort you out." Ryder walked out the bakery door, and Shelby didn't even bother arguing with him. There were a lot of things she didn't know and a lot of things she wasn't sure about, but she knew Ryder was good at what he did, and she knew she'd be an idiot not to let him do it.

She watched as he carried the cake outside, his

muscles rippling as he set the box in the back of the Hummer. He turned, his half smile making her stomach flip.

Everything about him made her stomach flip, her heart sing, her soul yearn.

If it had only been those things that drew her to him, she would have been fine. Chemistry, physical attraction, stick any name on it you wanted, and it was the same. Fleeting and shallow. Not something to build forever on.

But it *wasn't* only those things that drew her to him.

She *liked* Ryder.

Liked how he argued with Dottie, but still did what she asked. Liked the way he stuck to his promises and the way he lived his faith. Liked that he seemed to like her just the way she was. No trying to change her. No telling her she needed to be different. Just wanting her to be her.

That was a powerful gift to give someone, and Shelby didn't know if she had the strength to turn it away.

"Okay. We're set." He took her arm, led her into the cool spring day, his body shielding her from the street the way it always did, offering his life to keep her safe.

Another gift, and thinking about it made her throat clog and her heart beat faster.

"Ryder," she said as she climbed into the Hummer,

and he waited, his hand on the door, his eyes staring straight into hers.

"Yeah?"

"Thanks."

He nodded and closed the door.

Maybe he knew what she meant.

Maybe he didn't.

Hopefully, Shelby would have a chance to explain. Hopefully, neither of them would die before then.

She prayed they wouldn't, clutching the extra icing and box of flowers as Ryder pulled away from the bakery and headed for Manito Park.

NINETEEN

Watching Shelby work was an addiction Ryder couldn't afford to give in to. Not when her life depended on him staying focused.

He scanned the Japanese gardens as she covered a long table with a white cloth and set a fancy-looking silver cake stand on top of it. A hundred yards away, Darius watched the entrance of the gardens, his attention focused, his body taut. Knowing him, he was hoping for some action.

Ryder wanted nothing more than to get Shelby back to his place and lock her away there. She wasn't safe out in the open, and he should have refused to bring her to the park, but part of his job was to get clients where they needed to be and to keep them safe there. He'd done it dozens of times before, and this time shouldn't be any different.

Shelby made it different, though.

Protecting her was personal. Keeping her safe was personal.

He scanned the gardens again, his attention caught by a movement to his right. A man and his son passed by, probably heading home before dusk, the park's posted closing time.

He paced to a small bridge that arched over a stream, searching for signs of tampering, but his team had been thorough. The garden was pristine, the serenity of it tempting him to believe that everything would go just the way he'd planned.

Easy in.

Easy out.

No trouble.

The sun hung low in the sky, dusk falling as the park grew quiet and Shelby continued her work. Despite the peacefulness of the evening, Ryder's hackles were raised, his skin prickling as darkness spread through the garden.

A candlelit wedding was a nice idea unless someone wanted you dead. Then it became a hazard, shadows growing long and undulating in the evening breeze as a crew quietly set up rows of chairs and readied the gardens for the ceremony.

"Okay. That's it. It's as good as it's going to get." Shelby stepped away from the cake, completely oblivious to anything but her work, but Ryder felt something in the air, a breathless waiting quality that put him on edge.

Someone was watching.

He signaled Darius and Lionel Matthews, and they slid into the shadows, going on the hunt for the hunter.

"Good. Let's go." He took Shelby's hand, pulling

her away from the cake, Lincoln Stanley slipping into place behind them. One of the newest team members, Lincoln moved silently, weaving through the arriving wedding guests, then disappearing as he scouted the path back to the Hummer.

"I can't leave until the bride and groom get here. The cake—"

"No one is going to touch the cake, Shelby Ann, but I'm not liking the way things are starting to feel, so we're taking off."

"But—" She tried to protest, but he dragged her from the cake and across the small bridge.

Up ahead, Darius appeared, giving an all-clear signal and then slipping into thick woods beside the path. Something wasn't right. They both knew it. Ryder just hoped his men could find the threat before it found Shelby.

Darkness fell quickly as they made their way from the Japanese gardens into the lilac gardens. Manito Park had too many gardens, in Ryder's opinion. Too many places for someone to hide.

The sweet scent of lilac hung in the air as he led Shelby past deep purple bushes, light purple ones and white ones, their shadows long in the evening light. Everything peaceful, but not everything right. Something was about to go down, and if Ryder wasn't careful, it would take Shelby down with it.

"It's quiet," she whispered, and he nodded, probing shadows, studying dark corners, waiting, knowing.

The hair on the back of his neck stood on end,

and he hurried her to a ten-foot slate wall carved into the side of a steep hill. Lilac bushes pressed close to cold stone, and he shoved Shelby behind the thick branches and heavy boughs.

"Do you think—"

"Shh." He shushed her, listening to the silence. A twig cracked. Grass rustled. Then silence again, thick and expectant.

A loud blast rocked the air, a plume of smoke shooting up into the sky from the area they'd just left. The Japanese gardens or somewhere close to it. The caustic scent of explosives drifted through the lilac garden, filling Ryder's nose and throat and lungs. He expelled it and the memories of another time and another explosion.

"What was that?" Shelby cried, her eyes wide with shock, her face paper-white.

"Nothing I want you near. Stay there, and don't move until I say different."

"Where are you going?" She clutched his hand, her palm cool and dry, her grip tight and desperate.

"Nowhere." His operatives would check out the explosion. He needed to stay close, make sure he didn't let his guard down, lose his focus. The explosion was a distraction, a red herring designed to confuse.

"Then why are you leaving?"

"Because the perp knows we're together. I don't want him finding you because he sees me."

"But—"

"Stay put." He eased his hand from hers, his heart thudding hard and fast as he pulled his gun and moved away.

Dusk cast gray shadows across the garden, and he studied each one, willing the perp to walk into his line of sight.

His leg ached deep in the bone, a reminder of where he'd once been and where he didn't plan on ever being again. Helpless, hopeless, afraid. He'd fought back from it, found strength in himself and in his faith. Now, he needed to use both to keep Shelby alive.

A flash of movement to his left warned him seconds before a dark ball flew through the air.

He dived for cover, his body reacting before his brain registered the truth.

A grenade!

The world exploded, bits of earth and grass raining down, the force of the explosion knocking the breath from Ryder's lungs.

"Ryder!" Shelby screamed, jumping from her hiding place, racing toward him, her eyes shimmering blue in the evening gloom.

"Go back!" But it was too late. A soft pop. A bloom of red in a sea of lilac, and Shelby was falling. Another pop. Shouted words, but Ryder's only thought was Shelby. He ran toward her, his gun drawn and ready, his heart thundering with fear and anger.

"Shelby?" His hand shook as he touched the pulse

point in her neck, felt the thready, weak throb of her heart.

Blood bubbled up from a hole in the right side of her chest, seeping into her cotton shirt and spilling onto the ground.

Too much blood.

He'd failed her, and she might die because of it.

He pressed his hand against the wound, realized blood was seeping from beneath her back, too.

Something moved to his right, and he pivoted, aiming his gun at the figure that raced toward him.

"Hold your fire!" Darius called, and Ryder turned his attention back to Shelby. Her face devoid of color, her eyes closed, she had the grayish tinge of the dying.

Please, God, don't let her die.

"I've already called an ambulance. Hopefully, it'll be here soon. She's lost a lot of blood." Darius knelt beside him, frowning at the blood that stained the ground.

"Go find the guy who did this," Ryder said, unwilling to leave Shelby and unwilling to let her attacker escape.

"Matthews is after him. I got off one good shot when he bolted from his hiding place, and I'm pretty sure I hit him. He ran into the woods on that hill." He gestured to a hill a hundred yards out, covered with trees and shrouded in darkness.

"What about Lincoln?" Ryder pressed his jacket

against Shelby's wound, trying to staunch the flow of blood, trying to will the life to stay in her.

"Injured in an explosion near the reception site. Matthews was heading back to offer aid when the grenade was lobbed. We tried to get a bead on the perp, but he was behind a boulder, and I couldn't get off a shot until he ran."

"She's losing too much blood." Ryder spoke out loud, the words tasting like dust, his stomach twisting with fear. He should have been able to keep her from being hurt. Should have protected her.

Ryder pressed harder on the bubbling wound, his hand shaking.

"Shelby?" He leaned close, listening for her breath, hearing nothing.

"She's still breathing," Darius said, but the assurance did little to comfort Ryder. Breathing for now, but maybe not in a minute.

"We need that ambulance," he responded, and the sound of sirens seemed to answer, drifting from somewhere too far away.

Please, God, get it here in time.

"Come on, Shelby Ann. You're not going to die and leave Dottie to take care of the bakery, are you?"

"I was thinking about it." The words were so quiet, he wasn't sure he'd actually heard them.

"Then how about you think about something else?" He used his free hand to brush dirt from her cheek, and she opened her eyes but didn't speak.

"Shelby? What are you thinking about?" He persisted, because he was afraid if she stopped talking, she'd stop breathing.

"I'm thinking that I want to cry and that I shouldn't. I don't think I can afford to lose any more fluids." She tried to smile, and his heart responded, tightening in his chest, aching with a hot, throbbing pain.

If she died, he didn't think it would ever go away.

"It's okay to cry when you've been shot." He smoothed her hair, and she closed her eyes.

"You wouldn't cry. Not even if you were shot." Tears slipped down her cheeks, her blood still seeping through his coat, her skin growing even paler.

"Maybe not, but I'd cry if I lost you."

She opened her eyes, looked into his face. "I think I believe you."

"You should. I cried the day I found out my buddies were killed in that explosion in Afghanistan. You're not going to make me cry again, are you?"

"I'm not sure it's my choice, and I want you to know how sorry I am."

"For what?"

"I should have stayed where you asked me to. You're the best bodyguard I've ever had."

"I'm the *only* bodyguard you've ever had."

"If I'd had a million, you'd still be the best, and I should have listened to you. I'm the one who messed up. Not you. Remember that, okay?" Her hand dropped over his, the one that pressed his coat to the bullet wound, and his throat constricted.

He could not lose her.

"Where's that ambulance?" he barked, meeting Darius's concerned gaze.

"There!" Darius jumped up, racing toward the crew that ran toward them.

"Hang on. They're almost here," Ryder said, but Shelby's eyes were closed, her breathing shallow and raspy. "Shelby?"

"It's okay," she responded. "I'm not afraid to die. I just…really wanted to live a few more of my dreams first."

"You're not going to die."

"Tell Dottie that I trust her to run the bakery—"

"You are not going to die!" he nearly shouted as the EMTs crowded in, edging him out.

"Ryder!" Shelby grabbed his hand, her grip weak. "Stay with me. I don't want to be alone."

He wasn't sure if she meant go to the hospital alone or die alone, but he nodded, not trusting himself to speak.

Then he moved back and let the medics work.

TWENTY

Fading.

That's how dying felt. At least that's what Shelby figured it must feel like, and fading was exactly what she was doing. Drifting and fading and going away, but she didn't want to go. Not yet.

She groaned as she was lifted onto a gurney, the pain so intense she wanted to close her eyes and slip away, but she was afraid that if she did, she'd never find her way back.

"You're going to be okay, ma'am," a female EMT said, her nutmeg skin and dark eyes shimmering in the evening light.

Shelby wasn't sure if she was supposed to respond, but she couldn't seem to catch her breath, so she kept silent as someone jabbed her arm with a needle.

She barely felt it, barely felt anything. Just muted pain and panic that she might fall asleep and never wake up.

Please, God, I'm not ready to die.

Darkness edged in, and she fought it as the gurney bumped over grass and dirt, people talking, the sweet scent of lilac mixing with the coppery scent of blood, everything moving.

Flying.

No pain. Just darkness. Her heart pounding in her ears, in her chest. Her body vibrating with it.

Then nothing.

No fear.

No worries.

No dreams.

"You're not leaving me, are you, Shelby Ann?" a voice whispered from somewhere far away, and she wanted to ignore it, wanted to keep floating in nothingness.

"Shelby?" The tone captured her as the voice hadn't, the desperation in it tugging her back to pain and fear.

Too much effort to stay there.

To open her eyes.

To try to find the voice that called her name again.

Ryder's voice.

She wanted to reach for him, but her arms were leaden, her fingers numb.

"I'm not going to let you leave. Not before you have a chance to live those dreams." Warm words, warm breath against her ear, warm fingers twining with hers, all of it seeming to lighten her heavy lids.

She opened her eyes, stared into Ryder's concerned face, looked into his deep brown eyes.

She didn't want to leave any more than he wanted to let her go, but she had no voice to say the words, no energy to tell him she was going to stick around, so she just stared into his eyes as the ambulance sped to the hospital. Stared and stared and tried to lose herself in them instead of the darkness that wanted to sweep back over her.

"Okay, ma'am. We're here. Just relax and let us do all the work." The EMT patted her arm reassuringly, and then Shelby was moving away from Ryder. She tried to hold on to his hand, but her grip was weak, and it slipped from her grasp.

Wait! she tried to say, but no sound came out.

She was wheeled into a narrow, well-lit corridor, people shouting instructions and information that must have had something to do with her, but that she could make no sense of.

All her thoughts were foggy and thick, her thinking sluggish.

She heard words, but they were disjointed and unconnected.

Gunshot wound.

Blood loss.

Surgery.

Everything swirling and whirling in her ears, mixing with the erratic beat of her heart.

Dying.

That's what she was doing. Right there in the hospital.

"Sir, you're going to have to wait here!" a nurse

barked as she ran alongside the stretcher, her fingers on Shelby's wrist.

"I'll stay with her until you reach the operating room," Ryder responded, and Shelby tried to see him past the veil of clouds that seemed to be over her eyes.

"Sir—"

"I'm staying."

More voices. More words. Men and women in uniforms. Panic in the air.

Then everything quiet and still.

"This is it, sir. You can't go any farther."

"Shelby?" Ryder leaned so close she could see him through the clouds, count the flecks of gold in his brown eyes, see the blond stubble on his chin. Her heart beat hollowly, the light, airy feel of floating returning, but she reached out, touched his cheek.

"Don't leave me, Ryder."

"I have to," he responded, and she was sure his voice was shaking, but maybe *she* was shaking, her heart shimmering rather than beating.

"I'm so scared," she whispered, and Ryder brushed hair from her forehead, kissed her chilled skin.

"You're too brave to be scared, Shelby Ann."

"Only when you're with me. Please, don't leave me."

"You're plenty brave, even without me, but I'll be out here waiting, and I'll be here when you come out. The first person you see. I promise." He kissed her forehead again, his breath warming her cold, cold skin, and she thought there were tears in his eyes as he stepped away, but the fog had rolled in again, and she couldn't be sure.

"Everything is going to be fine, Shelby." A dark-haired man dressed in green scrubs patted her hand as she started to move again.

Flying.

Floating.

Fading.

Please, God, I don't want to leave my mother, my sister. I don't want to leave Dottie. I don't want to leave Ryder. Not before I know what we could have had together.

The prayer whispered through her mind as she floated into darkness.

TWENTY-ONE

She could die.

Ryder had seen it in Shelby's eyes and in her blue-tinged lips. She knew it, too.

Scared.

That's what she'd said, and he'd been scared, too.

Terrified that they'd roll her into the operating room and she wouldn't come out alive.

He was still terrified.

"How is she?" Darius jogged toward him, blood splattered across his white dress shirt, his face gaunt with worry.

"Not good. She's been in surgery for four hours already. Did Matthews get the perp?" Ryder ground the question out, and Darius shook his head.

"A K-9 unit was dispatched, and they're on his trail. The good news is, the one shot I got off hit him. The police found a few drops of blood on the ridge where the perp was hiding."

"The good news will be when he's in custody."

"It'll happen, Ryder."

"It should have happened before he got another

chance at Shelby," he said, anger at his failure beating hard in his chest.

"It's difficult to stop someone when you don't know who he is or where he is, and this guy is good at protecting himself. He planned things out perfectly today. An explosive device hidden ahead of time, and all he had to do was push a button to detonate it. He meant it to be a distraction, and he succeeded. We're fortunate more people weren't hurt."

"Aside from Lincoln and Shelby, were there other injuries?" Ryder asked, knowing that if there were, he'd be wearing another layer of guilt. His men had done a sweep of the area before he arrived with Shelby, covering a grid that encompassed nearly half an acre. They'd found nothing, but something had been there. That was his responsibility and failure as much as theirs.

"No. The bomb was in a copse of trees two hundred yards from the reception site. Our perp waited until we were moving away from the site, and then set it off. There wasn't a lot of force in the explosives. He obviously had only one target.

"And he found it. I should have been more careful." Ryder slammed his fist into the wall.

"You were as careful as anyone could be, and if Shelby hadn't left her cover—"

"It wasn't her fault."

"It wasn't *anyone's* fault. Accept that or you won't be able to help Shelby heal."

He was right.

Ryder knew that, and he took a deep breath. "What else have you got for me?

"Lincoln saw our perp moving through the trees right before the explosion. He gave chase, saw the guy climb into a car on the far side of the woods seconds before the explosion. A minute after the explosion, the perp tossed a grenade at you."

"I know. No need to rehash it," Ryder said wearily, and Darius frowned.

"You're not getting my point, boss. It would have taken more than a minute for the perp to run from that parking area to the ridge."

"You're saying we're dealing with two perps?" The knowledge shot through Ryder like raw adrenaline. His pulse jumped, his body hummed with it.

"Exactly."

"Ryder Malone?" A police officer strode toward him, grim-faced and timeworn, his gray hair shaggy and unkempt.

"Yes." Ryder met him halfway, and the officer offered a hand.

"I'm Detective Nick Jasper with the Spokane Police Department. I'd like to ask you a few questions about what happened this evening."

"Go ahead."

"We'll probably be more comfortable in a less public place. The hospital has provided its conference room. If you'll—"

"No."

"Excuse me?" Detective Jasper frowned.

"If you want to ask questions, ask them here. Otherwise, they'll have to wait."

"I don't think that's going to work for me, Mr. Malone."

"I don't think you have a choice." He walked back to the operating-room door, not swayed by Darius's subtle head gesture. He'd promised Shelby he'd be there when she came out, and he would be. Even if he had to stand there for the rest of the night.

"Okay. We'll do this your way." Detective Jasper stepped up beside him. "You visited Dr. Christopher Peterson this afternoon, correct?"

"That's an odd question to ask after a woman nearly died." Ryder eyed the detective, not sure where they were headed with the interview, but intrigued. He'd had a gut feeling about Peterson, and it hadn't been a good one.

"Not so odd seeing as how another woman visited him and died less than twenty-four hours later."

"Maureen Lewis?"

"That's right. You and Ms. Simons were digging into her death, right? Trying to find out who wanted to kill her and why."

"Because someone was also trying to kill Shelby." And had nearly succeeded. Might still succeed.

Please, Lord, don't let her die.

"I understand that, Malone. I know why you've been digging. I'd have done the same in your position, but you may have dug up more than any of us suspected. You've obviously made someone very, very uncomfortable."

"Right, and here's my question for you, Detective. What are you doing about it?"

"We've reopened the case files of the murders at Good Samaritan, and we're looking into Peterson's alibis again. We've also sent men out to question him regarding his whereabouts this evening. Your men reported two perps. If he doesn't have an alibi, it's possible he was one of them."

"And the other perp?"

"That's where things get interesting. The doctor has an old army buddy who just happens to be on our short list of persons of interest in the serial-arson case."

"That's just now coming out?"

"We had no reason to try to link Peterson to the arsonist before. Once we did, we started asking around. Wallace McGregor's name was mentioned in conjunction with the doctor. Several friends and even Peterson's wife reported that the two are as close as brothers. The thing is, Wallace is a retired firefighter. Retired because he set his own house on fire for the insurance money eleven years ago. His wife was sick at the time, and he said he was desperate for the money, so the judge let him off with probation."

"It sounds like you've got your man."

"Men, and we're going to build cases so strong they'll be in jail for the rest of their lives."

"Good." But Ryder only cared about one thing at that moment. Seeing Shelby, looking into her eyes, touching her warm skin.

Please, God, let her live.

"Is there anything else you need to discuss with me, Detective?" Ryder asked.

"We're done for now. We'll have guards posted 24/7 outside Ms. Simons's hospital room if she…" His voice trailed off, and he cleared his throat. "We'll make sure she stays safe until our suspects are rounded up."

"Thanks." Ryder didn't bother pointing out that they hadn't been successful in keeping her safe so far. No one had.

The thought pounded through his head and his heart, the guilt of letting her be hurt filling him up.

The operating-room door swung open, and a dark-haired man dressed in blood-spattered scrubs stepped out. He met Ryder's eyes, and the somberness of his gaze made Ryder's heart skip a beat. "I'm Dr. Griffon. Are you related to the patient?"

"I'm a friend. How is she?"

"Holding her own. We had to repair a torn artery, and her scapula is cracked, but she should make a full recovery. We've taken her to ICU. We'll be able to monitor her condition more carefully there."

"I'd like to speak with her as soon as possible," Detective Jasper said, and the doctor frowned.

"You may have to wait several days, Officer. She's in no condition to speak with anyone."

"It's *Detective* Jasper, and I understand that she needs to heal, but—"

"You heard the doctor, Detective. She can't speak with you," Ryder cut in, his eyes still on the surgeon.

"Here's my card. Give me a call as soon as she's able to." The detective handed Dr. Griffon his card, then walked away.

"I'd like to see her. Will that be possible?" Ryder asked, but he didn't plan to take no for an answer. He'd promised Shelby he'd be there when she came out of surgery, and he would be.

"Once she's settled in. The ICU is on the second floor. I'll have a nurse—"

An alarm sounded, the siren screaming through the corridor.

"Fire alarm!" the doctor shouted over the sound. "We'd better get out of here."

"What about Shelby?"

"The ICU staff know the procedure. She'll be wheeled to safety, but only if it's necessary."

Ryder barely heard the last few words—he was already on his way to the stairwell. Detective Jasper had promised 24/7 protection, but Ryder didn't know if guards were already stationed near the ICU.

And maybe that's what the alarm was all about.

Not a real fire, a distraction. Just like the explosion had been.

Ryder's heart raced as he bounded up two flights of stairs, brushing by a half-dozen people who were running to the exit. He burst out into the second-floor corridor, ignoring a nurse who motioned for him to leave.

The sign for the ICU was at the end of the corridor, and he ran against the current of people streaming toward the stairwell.

"You going in?" Darius shouted above the screaming alarm, and Ryder nodded, glad his friend had followed him up.

"Stay out here. If you see anyone coming this way, assume that he's trouble."

The alarm cut off as Ryder opened the door to the ICU.

Several nurses stood near a computer screen, monitoring patients as they spoke quietly to one another. They looked up as Ryder approached.

"Sir, you need to stay outside until the fire department gives us the all clear."

"I'm Shelby Simons's bodyguard," he responded, and the oldest of the group frowned.

"We were told she'd have police protection. No one mentioned a bodyguard. I'll check with security after the doctor finishes with her. Go ahead and have a seat." She gestured to a row of chairs near the nurses' station, but Ryder had no intention of sitting. He'd just seen Shelby's doctor, and he'd been on his way out of the hospital.

"What doctor?"

"Her family practitioner. Dr. Peterson."

"Peterson?" Ryder's blood went cold.

"Yes. Why?"

"What room is she in?"

"I—"

"What room?"

"Room 10. He walked in right before you got here. I—"

Ryder didn't listen. He ran.

TWENTY-TWO

Drowning.

Shelby fought as she sank like lead to the bottom of the deep end of the pool. Summertime in California, and she'd been swimming since before she could walk, but she couldn't push up from the bottom, couldn't reach the crisp, clear sky that hovered above the surface of the water.

She shoved against the bottom, but felt nothing. Not the hard cement of the public pool or the tile bottom of her grandmother's.

She flailed, trying to move her arms, her legs, but they were trapped, her face suddenly pressed into the mud at the bottom of the lake.

Lake?

Her eyes flew open, but she saw nothing, knew nothing but terror and deep, throbbing pain. She tried to scream, but she had no air to do it. Something pressed against her face so hard she thought her nose would break.

She shoved at the weight with her hands. Felt fluffy softness and crisp, cool fabric.

Pillow.

She dredged up the word from the depth of her oxygen-starved brain.

She was being smothered by a pillow.

Fight!

She tried to twist away, but couldn't free herself.

I'll be here when you come out.

Ryder's words seeped through the fog of her terror. When had he said them?

Where?

She couldn't hold on to the memories, wasn't sure if she'd really heard them—she only knew that she was about to die, and that when she did, she'd lose any chance of ever having all the things she'd once dreamed of.

Don't let your failures ruin your possibilities.

But she had.

Two strikes, and she'd been out.

But she didn't want to stay out.

She wanted to risk it all, try for number three and shoot for forever.

She bucked against the force that held her down, and suddenly, the pillow lifted.

Darkness gone.

Light and air drifting in.

Shelby gasped, pulling deep breaths of antiseptic-scented air into her lungs.

Something crashed into the side of her bed, jarring her out of the stupor she seemed to be in. Dark shadows wrestled across the floor, panted breaths carrying into the silent room.

She tried to scream, but her throat was raw and dry, and all that came out was a raspy cough. She coughed again and again, pain shooting up her back and chest and lodging in her neck.

"Calm down, Shelby Ann. You're going to pull out all the stitches the doctor spent so much time putting in." Ryder leaned over her, his eyes blazing, his cheek red and swollen.

Number three.

Forever.

The words whispered through her mind as she reached out to touch his injury, the IV in her hand tugging as she moved.

"What happened?"

"You were shot." He lifted her hand, gently kissed her knuckles.

"Not to me. To your cheek," she rasped, and he fingered the bruise.

"Dr. Peterson decided to pay you a visit. We had a disagreement about whether or not he was going to stay."

"He was trying to smother me," she said, and he nodded, glancing at the prone figure that lay a few feet from the bed.

"He won't get a chance to try again."

"Is he…?"

"Dead? No, but he may wish he was when he's thrown in jail."

"Is everything okay in here?" Two security guards raced into the room, Darius and a police officer right behind them.

"The guy on floor is Dr. Peterson, Detective Jasper. He was trying to smother Shelby when I walked into the room," Ryder responded, and the officer knelt beside Peterson, patting him down, then turning him over and placing handcuffs on his wrists.

"I guess we've proven our theory, Malone. Peterson really was behind all of this," he said as he pulled Dr. Peterson to his feet.

"I'm not behind anything. I was checking on my patient—"

"She's not your patient, and I'm not sure how pressing a pillow to her face counts as checking on her." Ryder rested a hand on Shelby's shoulder, his touch so light and comforting that her eyes closed, the pain in her chest and back easing as her muscles relaxed.

"I want a lawyer," Peterson responded, and Shelby thought about opening her eyes and looking into the face of the man who'd tried to murder her, but she couldn't manage it.

"You'll get a lawyer, Dr. Peterson, and once you have one, you'll probably be counseled to cooperate and tell us whether it was you or your buddy Wallace who murdered Maureen Lewis." The detective's voice was gruff and filled with irritation, but it sounded far away and muted, its urgency lost as

Shelby drifted further from the room and the pain, Ryder's hand all that anchored her to reality.

"Neither of us killed anyone."

"You're lying," Ryder growled.

"I'm not—"

"You might as well fess up, Doctor. Our K-9 team apprehended Wallace. He's already down at the station, singing like a canary."

"I don't know what you're talking about," the doctor insisted, and Shelby wanted to listen to the conversation, *really* listen, but she drifted instead, floating in a place halfway between reality and dreams.

"Shelby?" Ryder called her back, and she opened her eyes.

The room had emptied. No doctor. No guards. No police officer. Just Ryder.

Just the way it should be.

She smiled, because she didn't have the energy to speak, and he ran a finger along her cheekbone.

"You must have hit something when you fell. You're going to have a bruise."

"It's better than being dead." She forced the words past her raw throat.

"True." He poured water from a plastic pitcher, shoved a straw into a plastic cup and held it for her to sip. "Not too much. The doctor might not approve."

"Peterson?" she asked, her mind muddled, her thoughts confused.

"The guy who spent four hours stitching you up after I nearly let you be killed."

"You didn't. I did. I should have listened and stayed where you told me to."

"Why didn't you?" He brushed hair from her forehead, his touch tender and easy, his eyes dark and knowing.

"Because my life would be empty without you in it, and I was sure you were about to die. It made me realize something."

"Yeah? What's that?"

"Number three? It's forever. I wouldn't want to miss out on that."

"Me, neither." He smiled gently, and Shelby imagined seeing that smile in a year, in five years, in ten. She imagined seeing it when they were both old and gray and sitting in rocking chairs.

"You're smiling." Ryder traced the curve of her lips. "What are you thinking about?"

"Sunsets and sunrises and front-porch swings. With you."

"I like that idea, Shelby Ann," he responded. "I like it a lot."

"So, it's a date?" she asked, her muscles relaxing into a sleep she couldn't deny.

"Not a date, Shelby," he whispered close to her ear. "Every dream you've ever had. Every dream I've ever had. All of it finally coming true. Forever."

"I like that idea, Hercules," she said and felt his smile as he pressed a gentle kiss to her lips.

"Good. Now, stop talking and start resting."

She didn't have the energy to call him bossy, but he was.

Bossy.

Wonderful.

Heroic.

She saw the truth as she slipped deeper into dreams. Saw it so clearly she didn't know why she hadn't seen it before. Every path she'd walked, every disappointment, every heartache had led to Ryder. It was God's plan, and it was so much better than hers had been.

Her eyes drifted closed, and she didn't fight the darkness that pulled her into sleep. She knew she didn't need to. Ryder would be waiting when she woke.

Number three.

Forever.

EPILOGUE

Shelby leaned over the large sheet cake, piping a porch onto the house she'd painstakingly created. A two-story Tudor with a lush green lawn and a white picket fence. Every eave, every window, every fence post had been drawn, painted and shadowed to match her new home.

It had taken three days and a little more energy than she probably should have expended, but it looked great, and Shelby was pleased with the results.

"What do you think, Mazy? Pretty nice, huh?"

The dog barked in response, her shiny black nose pressed to the floor as she searched for crumbs.

"Exactly what I was thinking. We're just missing one thing." Shelby set the white icing bag on the kitchen counter and lifted another one. Brown this time. She piped a hanging swing on the porch.

Perfect!

"Shelby Ann Simons, I thought I told you to take a nap!" Dottie bustled into the kitchen, her voice dripping ire, her eyes filled with concern.

"My guests will be here in a few hours, and I wanted to make sure the cake was ready for the housewarming party."

"It's ready. Go to bed. And you—" she turned her attention to Mazy "—out back for a while." She scooped up the dog and plopped her on the back deck, surreptitiously slipping her an oversize dog treat in the process.

"You know the vet said Mazy needs to cut back."

"What does she know? That dog weighs less than my big toe. Now, go to bed. I'm making my famous potato salad for the party, and I don't want you trying to steal my recipe."

"How about I just go sit on the porch swing?" Shelby asked as Dottie shooed her out of the kitchen.

"I don't care what you do, girl. Just rest. You're never going to recover fully if you don't."

"I *am* fully recovered," Shelby responded, but they both knew it wasn't true. A serious staph infection after surgery had kept Shelby in the hospital for over a month. Five weeks later, she still tired easily, but she wasn't going to let that stop her from celebrating her new home. Local contractors had moved heaven and earth to build it quickly, and she'd finally moved in. She loved the new house. Free of bad memories and broken dreams, it was waiting to be filled with wonderful new ones.

She hummed a little as she walked onto the front porch and sat on the swing, closing her eyes and letting the warm summer air wrap around her.

"Have I told you lately how beautiful you are?" Ryder's voice flowed over her, and she opened her eyes, watching as he took the porch stairs two at a time.

"Every day, but I don't mind if you tell me again."

"You're beautiful. You also look tired. Dottie said you worked seven hours today."

"Dottie has a big mouth."

"I heard that," Dottie called through the screen door.

"The doctor said part-time for another week or two, remember?" Ryder settled on the swing beside her, and she scooted in close, sliding her arm around his waist and resting her head on his shoulder. He smelled of outdoors and sunshine and everything she loved most.

"I love you so much, Ryder," she said as he stroked her hair.

"I love you, too, but you're not going to distract me. You can't work seven hours yet. You need more time to recover."

"I'm ready to get back to my life. That means pushing myself sometimes."

"Push a little, but don't overdo it, okay?" His hand skimmed over her hair again, slid down her arm and back up, the caress filling her with longing. Ryder was everything she'd been searching for, every dream she'd given up on, and her heart swelled with love for him.

"For you, I'll try not to overdo it."

"Good, because fall is coming, and it's my favorite time of year."

"Mine, too," she murmured sleepily. Much as she wanted to go back to her full work schedule, she had to admit, seven hours had been too much. Her eyelids were heavy, her muscles warm and relaxed. She thought she could sit where she was forever, her head on Ryder's shoulder, his hand sliding up and down her arm.

"I'm glad we agree, because now that I've taught you how to fire a handgun, I think it's time for you to teach me how to make a cake."

"That's fair," she responded, snuggling closer and closing her eyes. "What kind of cake do you want to make? Chocolate? Red velvet? Banana?"

"Wedding."

"Wedding?" She straightened, suddenly wide-awake. "Do you know how difficult wedding cakes are to make? How much time they take? We should probably start with something simpler. A birthday cake or—"

"It's not just any wedding cake I want to make with you." He fished in his pocket, pulled out a blue velvet jeweler's box and opened it to reveal a sparkling sapphire set in a simple platinum band.

"Ryder—"

"You've owned my heart from the first time I saw you smile. Almost losing you nearly tore me in two. You've been given a second chance. *We've* been given one, and I don't want to waste a minute of it. Will you marry me?"

"I—"

"Say yes, girl. Or I'll say it for you," Dottie hollered, and Ryder smiled.

"If Dottie's response is all I can get, I'll take it, but I'd rather hear it from you. *Will* you spend the rest of your life with me, Shelby Ann?"

"Yes," she whispered, tears sliding down her cheeks as he slipped the ring on her finger.

And then she was in his arms, every breath, every heartbeat in tune with his.

She slid her hands through his hair, loving the thickness of it, loving the velvety roughness of his jaw as her fingers trailed along warm skin, drifted along granite shoulders encased in crisp, cool cotton and settled over his heart.

"Don't make me bring a broom out there," Dottie called, and Ryder broke away, his breathing uneven, his eyes burning into Shelby's.

"I wasn't kidding about a wedding cake—a fall wedding cake."

"*This* fall?" Shelby asked as he tugged her to her feet.

"Would you rather wait until next year?" He pressed kisses along the column of her throat, his lips warm and firm and wonderful, and Shelby sighed.

"No."

"Good." He smiled down into her eyes, offering her everything she'd ever wanted and so much more than she'd ever imagined she would have. Two paths had converged and merged, God guiding and leading, prodding and pushing Shelby and Ryder straight into each other's hearts.

And Shelby was so very thankful that He had.

"Come on," she said. "If we're going to make our wedding cake together, we'd better start practicing now."

She led Ryder into the kitchen, glad to see that Dottie had made herself scarce. The piping bags were still on the counter, and she handed Ryder the white icing. "Let's get started."

"We may not want to practice on your house-warming cake, Shelby Ann. I'm not sure how well I'm going to take to this," he said, and she smiled, covering his hands with hers, guiding him as they wrote two words on the seat of the swing: *Three Forever.*

"What do you think?" she asked, looking into his dark chocolate eyes, seeing his love written there. True and real and selfless, the most wonderful gift any person had ever given her.

"I think," he said, scanning her face, his gaze dropping to her white polo shirt, her faded jeans, "it's perfect."

"*Absolutely* perfect," she responded, and he pulled her into his arms, kissed her until nothing else existed.

"So, how about we start planning this fall shindig? I've got a dozen bridal magazines. Let's start looking through them." Dottie slammed a pile of magazines on the kitchen table, and Shelby jumped back.

"Dottie!"

"What?" she asked with a sly smile.

"Do you plan to always have bad timing?" Ryder grumbled.

"Not always. Just until you two get to the I-dos," she responded, and he laughed.

"What do you think, then, Shelby Ann? Should we hurry up and get there?" he asked, pulling out a chair and gesturing for her to sit.

"You know" she responded, grabbing a magazine, her heart racing with the depth of her love for him, "I think that we should."

* * * * *

Dear Reader,

I used to believe that a smooth journey meant I was on the right road. When things were going well, I felt confident in who I was and where I was heading. When they weren't, I doubted my path and worried that I was stepping outside of God's will. That isn't the way life works, though. Sometimes, the best path is the most difficult one. Sometimes, to find where we are meant to be, we must struggle and fight and persist through tough times. That is the lesson Shelby Simons must learn when her good friend is murdered and she becomes the next target. Shelby must depend on security contractor Ryder Malone to keep her safe, but she has been hurt one too many times, and trusting Ryder isn't something she thinks she can ever do. The easy path means running from him and from the danger that is stalking her, but it is the difficult path that will bring her to the place she belongs.

I hope you enjoy the newest book in the Heroes for Hire series!

I love connecting with readers. You can visit me on Facebook or email me at shirlee@shirleemccoy.com.

Blessings,

Shirlee McCoy

Questions for Discussion

1. By the world's standards, Shelby is successful. What are her thoughts about the way her life is going?

2. Why do you think Shelby has had so many bad experiences when it comes to love?

3. Shelby has always dreamed of having a forever kind of love, but every time she shoots for it, she's disappointed. How does that impact her relationship with Ryder?

4. Shelby notices Ryder the first time he walks into her bakery, but she's already made the decision to stay single. What has she based that decision on?

5. Do you think her reasons for giving up on her dreams are valid? Explain.

6. Ryder has stopped looking for love, but he's not afraid to go after it when he meets Shelby. What is it about her that makes him think he might have finally found a person he can share his life with?

7. Shelby comes from a family of women who don't hold much stock in marriage or relation-

ships, but she has always wanted those things. Why do you think that is?

8. Nearly dying changed Ryder's perspective on life and made him value family and relationships more. What experiences have you had that have changed the way you view life? How has that changed your relationships?

9. Shelby and Ryder are obviously physically attracted to each other. What are the deeper reasons that they are drawn together?

10. Sometimes our plans aren't the same as God's plans for us. Have you ever had to change your course to fall in line with God's plan for your life?

11. How does Shelby's relationship with God impact her relationship with Ryder?

12. How important do you think it is for two people to share a common bond of faith?

LARGER-PRINT BOOKS!

GET 2 FREE
LARGER-PRINT NOVELS
PLUS 2 FREE
MYSTERY GIFTS

Love Inspired®

SUSPENSE
RIVETING INSPIRATIONAL ROMANCE

Larger-print novels are now available...

YES! Please send me 2 FREE LARGER-PRINT Love Inspired® Suspense novels and my 2 FREE mystery gifts (gifts are worth about $10). After receiving them, if I don't wish to receive any more books, I can return the shipping statement marked "cancel". If I don't cancel, I will receive 4 brand-new novels every month and be billed just $4.99 per book in the U.S. or $5.49 per book in Canada. That's a saving of at least 23% off the cover price. It's quite a bargain! Shipping and handling is just 50¢ per book in the U.S. and 75¢ per book in Canada.* I understand that accepting the 2 free books and gifts places me under no obligation to buy anything. I can always return a shipment and cancel at any time. Even if I never buy another book, the two free books and gifts are mine to keep forever.

110/310 IDN FEH3

Name	(PLEASE PRINT)	
Address		Apt. #
City	State/Prov.	Zip/Postal Code

Signature (if under 18, a parent or guardian must sign)

Mail to the **Reader Service:**
IN U.S.A.: P.O. Box 1867, Buffalo, NY 14240-1867
IN CANADA: P.O. Box 609, Fort Erie, Ontario L2A 5X3

Not valid for current subscribers to Love Inspired Suspense larger-print books.

**Are you a current subscriber to Love Inspired Suspense books
and want to receive the larger-print edition?
Call 1-800-873-8635 or visit www.ReaderService.com.**

* Terms and prices subject to change without notice. Prices do not include applicable taxes. Sales tax applicable in N.Y. Canadian residents will be charged applicable taxes. Offer not valid in Quebec. This offer is limited to one order per household. All orders subject to credit approval. Credit or debit balances in a customer's account(s) may be offset by any other outstanding balance owed by or to the customer. Please allow 4 to 6 weeks for delivery. Offer available while quantities last.

Your Privacy—The Reader Service is committed to protecting your privacy. Our Privacy Policy is available online at www.ReaderService.com or upon request from the Reader Service.

We make a portion of our mailing list available to reputable third parties that offer products we believe may interest you. If you prefer that we not exchange your name with third parties, or if you wish to clarify or modify your communication preferences, please visit us at www.ReaderService.com/consumerchoice or write to us at Reader Service Preference Service, P.O. Box 9062, Buffalo, NY 14269. Include your complete name and address.

LISUSLP11B

LARGER-PRINT BOOKS!

**GET 2 FREE
LARGER-PRINT NOVELS
PLUS 2 FREE
MYSTERY GIFTS**

Love Inspired®

Larger-print novels are now available...

YES! Please send me 2 FREE LARGER-PRINT Love Inspired® novels and my 2 FREE mystery gifts (gifts are worth about $10). After receiving them, if I don't wish to receive any more books, I can return the shipping statement marked "cancel". If I don't cancel, I will receive 6 brand-new novels every month and be billed just $4.99 per book in the U.S. or $5.49 per book in Canada. That's a saving of at least 23% off the cover price. It's quite a bargain! Shipping and handling is just 50¢ per book in the U.S. and 75¢ per book in Canada.* I understand that accepting the 2 free books and gifts places me under no obligation to buy anything. I can always return a shipment and cancel at any time. Even if I never buy another book, the two free books and gifts are mine to keep forever.

122/322 IDN FEG3

Name _____ (PLEASE PRINT)

Address _____ Apt. #

City _____ State/Prov. _____ Zip/Postal Code

Signature (if under 18, a parent or guardian must sign)

Mail to the Reader Service:
IN U.S.A.: P.O. Box 1867, Buffalo, NY 14240-1867
IN CANADA: P.O. Box 609, Fort Erie, Ontario L2A 5X3

Not valid to current subscribers to Love Inspired Larger-Print books.

**Are you a current subscriber to Love Inspired books
and want to receive the larger-print edition?
Call 1-800-873-8635 or visit www.ReaderService.com.**

* Terms and prices subject to change without notice. Prices do not include applicable taxes. Sales tax applicable in N.Y. Canadian residents will be charged applicable taxes. Offer not valid in Quebec. This offer is limited to one order per household. All orders subject to credit approval. Credit or debit balances in a customer's account(s) may be offset by any other outstanding balance owed by or to the customer. Please allow 4 to 6 weeks for delivery. Offer available while quantities last.

Your Privacy—The Reader Service is committed to protecting your privacy. Our Privacy Policy is available online at www.ReaderService.com or upon request from the Reader Service.

We make a portion of our mailing list available to reputable third parties that offer products we believe may interest you. If you prefer that we not exchange your name with third parties, or if you wish to clarify or modify your communication preferences, please visit us at www.ReaderService.com/consumerchoice or write to us at Reader Service Preference Service, P.O. Box 9062, Buffalo, NY 14269. Include your complete name and address.

LILP11B

ReaderService.com

You can now manage your account online!

- Review your order history
- Manage your payments
- Update your address

We've redesigned the Reader Service website just for you.

Now you can:

- Read excerpts
- Respond to mailings and special monthly offers
- Learn about new series available to you

Visit us today:

www.ReaderService.com

RS10